SIDELINES

PART ONE

J Ware

ISBN-13: 978-1-950650-33-0

Prologue

JAEDA

Devonte walked into the sandwich shop and then looked around; he was looking for his fiancée. He slightly nodded his head to the few customers that were in there and then continued to look around for Jaeda. He spotted her sitting at a table with another guy; they seemed as if they were in the middle of a comical conversation. He sighed and then walked over to the table; he stopped and they both looked up at him. Jaeda stopped laughing and then cleared her throat, as the guy did the same.

Devonte looked from Jaeda and then to the tall, dark, and seemingly handsome guy sitting with his fiancée. "Hey, baby…am I interrupting something?" Jaeda looked at the gentlemen sitting at the table with her and then back to Devonte. "Actually no, this man is gonna help us with the shop. This is Gordon and he's a potential investor. I'ma get back behind the counter, so you can talk to him." Before Devonte could say another word, Jaeda stood from the chair and then shook hands with Gordon. Afterwards, she smiled at both men and then went back to work.

Devonte looked around and then sat down in the chair that Jaeda had just gotten up from; he looked at Gordon and then nodded. "Potential investor, huh? Is that what you calling yourself now?" Gordon rolled his eyes and then slightly laughed. "Whatever, man; if you don't want her to know the truth, then stick to my lie, so we can move on..." Devonte sighed and then nodded; both men then began to talk.

Jaeda Arcadia and Devonte Sampson, were fifteen-year-old high school sweethearts when they met; there was an instant attraction and they were joined at the hip ever since. Devonte came from money; his parents, although vindictive at times, wanted more for their son. They wanted him to attend college and although it was a thought in his mind at first, he wanted to help Jaeda pursue her dream of owning her own business, preferably a restaurant. Both were great cooks, but Jaeda wanted to start small first; she believed once they were able, then they would be able to open a restaurant together. The sandwich shop was her idea of starting off small; not only various types of sandwiches were prepared there, but also various types of soups, desserts, and coffee.

Devonte's parents scoffed at this ridiculous dream of Jaeda's and were even more disgusted that their son would be a part of it. Devonte went against his parent's disapproval of all of this and decided to stand by his now fiancée's, side. Both were young, at the age of twenty, but sure about what they wanted; they knew that they wanted to be together forever. Devonte proposed on graduation night, but to Devonte's dismay, his parents were not going to pay for a wedding that they didn't approve of, so both youngsters were on their own. They decided to wait until they could afford to get married. Jaeda didn't come from money, so she had almost always been on her own; her mother died when she was seventeen from a drug overdose and her father was unknown to her, so Jaeda bounced back and forth from relative's homes until graduation. She and Devonte moved in together a year after he proposed.

*   *   *

Later that night and at home in their apartment, Jaeda was getting ready for bed when she saw Devonte sitting on the bed while going through papers. He was frustrated and sighed several times. Jaeda went to take her shower and then afterwards, she exited the bathroom to find that Devonte was still on the bed and going over papers that she assumed had to do with the sandwich shop. She sighed and then walked over to the bed; she called his name and he ignored her. She repeated herself and he finally looked up at her, as he aggressively spoke. "Yeah, baby…what?" She got in the bed and he followed her with his eyes.

Jaeda sighed. "We're gonna be alright with the shop; Corrina said she'd work a few days out the week part-time to help out and I can do more promotion, so…" He frowned, as he stopped her. "Baby, getting your best friend to work during the week is not gonna save us. We don't need more promotion either…we're drowning in debt. I mean, maybe this was…" Devonte stopped talking and then cleared his throat but Jaeda received the point he was making, clearly. She looked down and then slightly laughed even though there was nothing funny. She looked back up again and then at him. The look on his face said that he regretted what he was about to say before he stopped talking.

Jaeda shook her head. "Maybe this was, what? Go ahead and say it…maybe this was a bad idea in the first place; or maybe your parents were right from the beginning. I didn't put a gun to your head and make you do anything, Devonte. I said, this was something I wanted to do; you didn't have to be a part of this." He shook his head. "Right, Jaeda…I didn't have to do this, huh? You know we wouldn't be together if I went to college, so yeah, I had to do this."

Devonte angrily pushed the papers off the bed and was about to go to sleep; he was in the middle of rolling over on his side when she stopped him, by grabbing his arm. "What the hell is that supposed to mean?" He sighed and then rolled back over, aggressively; he looked at her and although he was reluctant to say anything, she was making him mad. "It means that you would of broke up with me if I went to college, so I stayed for you. You think I didn't have dreams? I know what my parents said, but I love you and that's why I wanted to do this with you…I didn't wanna lose you, but we're drowning, baby, and without my parent's support, I don't know how we're gonna make it." Before she could speak, he did again "I love you, baby…goodnight." Devonte was able to roll over this time and go to sleep.

Jaeda sat there and slightly threw her hands up. She was aware of their financial issues but had faith that they would overcome this and make the sandwich shop successful again, so they could further expand and finally open up a restaurant. She decided not to think about it anymore. She was going to the bank in the morning to see if she and Devonte could get a loan for their business. Jaeda turned the light off and then went to bed too, with hopes that she and Devonte would be alright.

Chapter 1

Five years later…

Rendell was in his office and working on a case; there was a knock at his door and he told whoever it was to come in. The door opened and Rendell looked up to see his eighteen-year-old son walk in. "I'm busy, Dell, so what do you want?" Rydell rolled his eyes and then closed the door, before walking over to his dad's desk. He stopped and then put his hands in his pockets. "I need to know about my car; like when you gonna buy it for me?" Rendell frowned and then sat back against his chair, as he stared at his obviously spoiled son. "What car are you talking about?" Rydell rolled his eyes again. "Come on now, dad; your wife let it slip that you were getting me a car…you know, the wife that's young enough to be my girlfriend."

Rendell cleared his throat. "She's not young enough to be your girlfriend and she's the only mama you've ever known, so show some respect for once. She probably only told you, to get on your good side, so you'd like her. After five years I think she's done a pretty good job at helping to raise you and your little brother." Rydell sighed and then nodded.

Although he was thirteen when he met his dad's new girlfriend, who soon became his stepmother, Rydell was still reluctant to let her in his life. His biological mother died when he was three and he didn't remember her. Rydell wasn't ready to let any woman in his dad's life or his. After his little brother came along, Rydell decided to accept his stepmother, even with her and his dad's ten-year age difference.

Rydell sighed. "Yeah, alright dad, you know I was just playing anyway, but uh, the car situation. Am I gonna get it before graduation or the day of?" Rendell put his hand over his face and then dropped it; he then looked at his son. "You're killing me, Dell, but you can get your car before graduation. I have something special planned for me and your mama that night, so while you're partying and your little brother is at your aunt's house, me and your mama are gonna have our night alone together. Now get out of here and drive your used car to your aunt's house to pick up Ju." Rydell slightly laughed and then nodded; he told his dad, goodbye, and then left to go pick up his three-year-old little brother, Rendell Murphy Jr., who everyone called, Ju. Afterwards, Rendell got back to work.

Chapter 2

Later that evening, Rydell returned home with Ju and found his stepmother, Journee, starting dinner. Journee turned around and smiled when she saw the boys; she bent down and picked up Ju. She stood back up and looked at Rydell, as he spoke. "It smells good, Journee…my dad can't cook worth a damn, but you know that already. Remember when he tried to impress you and cook Thanksgiving for all of us?" Journee laughed and Rydell did too.

Journee shook her head. "Well, thanks for the compliment and yeah, I remember that clearly. I had to clean up the mess your daddy made…I think we were the only people in the world to have Thanksgiving at midnight." Both laughed again and then Journee put Ju down. She then gave Ju a cookie from the pan that she let cool on the counter; afterwards, she got back to the stove.

Rydell hesitated and was about to leave the kitchen, but then stopped. He turned back around to his stepmother. "Hey, Journee…" She turned around and looked at Rydell, as he spoke. "You know I just be messing with you, right? My dad gets on me about respecting you, but I do respect you…you make him happy and you been a good mama to me, so I just wanted to let you know that." Journee slightly smiled and then nodded. "I get it, Dell. I know you respect me and I know how hard it was for you to accept me, but I love your daddy…I love you and Ju too. So, how mad was your daddy when you told him, I told you about the car?"

Rydell laughed and then stopped. "Ok, he wasn't mad…you know he don't get mad at you. He said, I'ma get my car before graduation though. I'ma head out in a little bit, so I'll see you later." Journee nodded and then watched as Rydell left the kitchen. Journee got back to cooking and tending to Ju. The doorbell rang and Journee left the kitchen to see who was at the door; she reached the door and then opened it to find Rendell's baby sister, Meela. "Hey girl, what's going on? I thought you were coming by tomorrow?" Meela made her way inside the house. Journee closed the door behind her and then the women talked on their way to the kitchen. "Yeah, well, after Dell picked up Ju, I had to come over and tell you about this new guy I'm talking to."

Journee stopped walking and then turned around to Meela. "A new guy? Every time I talk to you, you're talking about a new guy. So, what's going on with this new dude? He got kids, no kids, a baby mama…a wife…" Meela stopped Journee and then laughed. "Whatever, Journee…I just been testing the waters a little to find Mr. Right. We only been out a few times, but you know how Ren is. I can't tell him anything about any guys I date; he still thinks I'm a child sometimes." The women walked to the kitchen and then Meela sat down on the stool at the kitchen island. She smiled at Ju and then watched as he got up and ran out the kitchen to go play.

As Meela watched him, she smiled; her smile faded when she turned her head back towards Journee. "Journee, you alright?" Journee had her hand on her forehead; she removed it and then looked at Meela. "Yeah, I'm alright…I got a damn migraine or something." Meela slightly leaned her head to the side and then cleared her throat. "Migraine, huh? You pregnant or something? I mean, you been acting sickly for a while now…I didn't think y'all wanted more kids, but uh…" Journee stopped Meela from saying anything else. "No, I'm not pregnant; it's this graduation stuff that Ren got me doing for Dell. I just got through with Ju's birthday party and our anniversary is coming up. I think Ren is cheating on me…"

Meela laughed at Journee's last statement; she thought it was a joke. She realized that Journee wasn't laughing with her, so Meela stopped and then frowned. "I get all the stress, but are you serious? You know damn well Ren loves you; if anything, he probably thinks you're cheating on him. Did you forget he's about to be thirty-five and you're twenty-five? You remember the song, "The Men all pause"? That's you…and me, but I'm not married, so they can pause for me."

Journee slightly laughed at her sister-in-law and then shook her head. She sighed, as Meela stopped joking and then became serious. "Look, Journee…after Dell's mama died, I never thought Ren would find somebody else and settle down again, but he found you. We all were a little skeptical that it was gonna work because of the age difference, but you're not like all the others he dated, who wanted him for his money. Don't worry about anything and slow down with all your wifely duties…he loves the hell out of you." Journee smiled and then nodded; she thought her sister-in-law was right, but couldn't help the overwhelming feeling that something was wrong and Rendell was cheating on her. Regardless, Journee was overdoing everything and had to slow down before she burned herself out.

As she and Meela started to talk again, some time had passed. Dinner was ready and Rendell walked in the kitchen just in time; he greeted his sister and then smiled at his wife. He walked over to Journee and then gave her a kiss, as Meela rolled her eyes. "Hey, baby; the food smells good. Uh, can we talk?" Journee's smile faded and then she glanced at Meela. Meela frowned and then shook her head vigorously. "Ah hell no, Ren…seriously? You're really cheating on Journee? I thought she was just being paranoid, but damn. All those hoes you tried to bring around Dell and now that you got a good one, you're cheating on her."

Rendell frowned and then stared at his sister as if she were crazy; he then looked back at his wife. "What the hell? You think I'm cheating on you? You told my sister I was cheating on you?" Journee put her hand up to stop Rendell and then dropped it; she looked at Meela and gave her a look. Afterwards, Meela put both her hands up and said she was leaving. Rendell thought that was a good idea at this point.

After Meela left, Rendell turned back to his wife, as she spoke. "It's a misunderstanding, Ren…I'm just stressed and with my new job I'm starting in a week. I'm just running myself crazy." Rendell sighed and then put his arms around Journee's waist. "I'm not cheating on you and I'd never do that; I love you and everything I do is for you and this family. I just wanted to talk to you about our anniversary." Journee smiled and thought now that she was being ridiculous. "Yeah, you're right and I'm sorry." Rendell nodded and then they kissed. Afterwards, they got ready for dinner. Rendell went to get Ju and shortly after, Rydell returned home. The family sat down not too long after and ate dinner together.

Chapter 3

It was a week later and the day of Rydell's graduation. There was chaos in the Murphy household; Rydell was presented with his new car for his graduation gift and loved it. Journee, Meela, and Ju were together at the mall and shopping, while Rendell was at work and getting a little bit more done before Rydell's graduation.

As the women were out shopping, they stopped at the food court to have lunch. Journee's migraines had gotten worse over the course of the week and she had to get pain medication from the doctor. Meela looked at Journee, as they sat at the table and ate; she saw Journee rubbing her temples with her fingers. "Damn, maybe you need to go to the doctor again for the migraines. You don't look good…" Journee removed her fingers from her forehead and then looked at Meela; she looked at Ju and he was eating his food. Journee stood from the chair and looked at Meela again. "Uh, I'ma go get some water…maybe it'll help." Meela nodded and then watched Journee walk away.

As this was happening, there was someone else watching Journee at the same time. Meela noticed and frowned; at first, she thought she was mistaken, but it was clear now that Journee was being watched. As Journee was at the counter, she was about to ask for a cup of water when her migraine became worse; it nearly brought her down to her knees. Meela saw and quickly reacted; she got up from the table and then grabbed Ju from his chair. Meela hurried over to the counter and asked Journee if she was alright.

Journee stood upright, while using the counter to hold her steady; she nodded her head, even though it was obvious she wasn't alright at all. She said she wanted to go home and Meela thought that was a good idea. Meela helped Journee back to the table and then gathered their things. Afterwards, they left the mall.

When they got to the house, Meela told Journee to take some more pain medication and take a nap before Rydell's graduation; Journee complied and went upstairs, while Meela watched Ju.

Time passed and it was later that evening; Journee woke up and saw darkness because all the curtains were closed. She rose in the bed and then looked around while confused. Journee slowly got out of the bed and then once again looked around; she then left the bedroom.

Rendell came home and found the house eerily quiet, but then walked further into the house to hear Ju in the living room. He walked in the living room and smiled when he saw his son; he looked around and didn't see Journee or Rydell. He yelled for either of them, but only received one answer. Rydell came from down the hall and Meela came from upstairs; they both headed to the living room and then stopped at the same time.

Rydell looked at his aunt and then at his dad; he stood there and put his hands in his pockets, as Rendell looked between both of them. "What's going on? Dell…why aren't you getting ready?" Meela started to stutter and then stopped. Rendell stepped closer to both of them. "What's wrong, Meela? Where's Journee?" Meela sighed and then shrugged her shoulders. "I don't know, Ren…we went shopping earlier and her migraine started again, so we came home. I told her to take a nap before the graduation and I think she did. I mean, she went upstairs and I didn't hear from her again. That was three hours ago and now she's gone."

Rendell stared at his sister as if she were crazy; he looked at his son and then back to his sister. "What the hell do you mean, she's gone? Gone where?" Neither had a reasonable answer for him, and were frankly scared to tell him that his wife was gone or missing.

Meela sighed. "I don't know, Ren, but we been looking for her all over the house and she's not here. Her cell phone is still on the nightstand and nothing else is gone, so maybe she had to run an errand or something before the graduation." Meela didn't know what to think about all of this either but couldn't explain where Journee was. Rendell started to panic since Journee never went anywhere without her cell phone and he saw her SUV parked outside, so he was extremely worried about where his wife was. Rydell's graduation was starting in an hour and a half and he knew Journee wouldn't miss it.

Rendell shook his head from side to side. "No, no…something happened, something bad must have happened. She wouldn't just up and leave for no reason and not take her cell phone or her damn vehicle. Did she call a cab or walk away? I don't…" Rydell stopped his dad, since it seemed to them that he was about to have a nervous breakdown. "Dad, just calm down; I'ma get ready for my graduation and then head out. She probably had to make a run real fast or something. I'll keep my phone on vibrate so call me when you find her."

Rendell nodded and then watched Rydell jog upstairs to go get ready. Meela looked at Ju and then at her brother. "Uh hey, I'ma get Ju ready and you do whatever you have to, to find Journee in the meantime. Dell was right, so just calm down; she'll be back in time for his graduation." Rendell sighed and then took a deep breath; Meela grabbed Ju's hand and then took him upstairs to get him cleaned up and ready. Afterwards, Rendell took his cell phone from his pocket and made a few calls.

Chapter 4

Rydell was standing with his graduating class on the football field and in a line. Rendell and Meela were sitting on the bleachers and Ju was on his daddy's lap. Rendell kept looking around, as if Journee was going to show up at any minute; at least that's what he hoped would happen. They still hadn't heard from Journee and Rendell didn't know what to do; he was undecided about whether to report her missing or wait a little longer. Meela could tell that her brother was beyond worried and wished she could help him, but she honestly didn't know what she could do either. It was difficult since Journee didn't take her vehicle or her cell phone with her. Even her last call on her phone was of no significance since it was to Rendell, much earlier in the day.

The graduation started and Rendell had enough; he turned his head to Meela. "I can't take this anymore; she wouldn't miss Dell's graduation, so I'm filing a missing person's report after the graduation." Meela sighed and then nodded. Since her brother was going to file a missing person's report, then it meant that Journee's disappearance was real and this was really happening. She agreed with her brother and then they finished watching the graduation.

After the graduation, Rendell and Meela headed home with Ju and waited for the police. Rendell didn't tell Rydell what was going on or what he was going to do. When they were settled at home, they waited for the police to arrive. Meela took Ju upstairs and got him ready for bed, while Rendell sat in the living room and waited. He sat there and thought about the special evening he had planned for his and Journee's anniversary. All thoughts were running through his head; he thought about her concern a week before in regards to him cheating on her. He hoped she wasn't cheating on him and left him for another man.

Rendell heard the door and then snapped out of his trance; he stood from the chair and then walked out the living room. He saw Rydell and was about to say something when the doorbell rang. Rendell walked around his son and then opened the door to find the police. After the two police officers walked inside, Rendell started to explain what was going on and Rydell stood there with a frown on his face. He didn't know what he walked into. He had his cap and gown in his car and came home to see about his stepmother.

Rydell walked away from his dad and went to the living room; he didn't want to hear anymore. Meela came downstairs shortly after and both waited together; she told her nephew briefly that Rendell was going to report Journee, missing. Rendell gave the officers his wife's cell phone and the keys to her SUV to search; he wanted them to do all they could, but they suspected that it was just an unhappy wife that left her husband. Regardless, they would file the report and get back to Rendell.

Rendell slowly stepped into the living room after some time passed and then stood there; Rydell and Meela turned their heads to him and then stood from the couch. Rendell cleared his throat and then put his hands in his pockets. "I filed a report and even though they said they'd do everything to find her, I don't believe them. They think she left me of her own free will, but I'm gonna get my private investigator on it; I'll call him tonight. I'm sorry, Dell, that Journee missed your graduation. I'm gonna go lay down." Rydell nodded, as Meela sighed. After Rendell left the living room, Meela told Rydell, goodnight, and he gave his aunt a hug. Rydell was going out after his graduation to a party, but with Journee missing, he wasn't in the partying mood anymore; he decided to stay in and be there for his dad and little brother.

Chapter 5

Another week had gone by and Rendell was at work; it had been hard staying sane and concentrating when his wife was still missing. The police had no luck and Rendell suspected they wouldn't. Rendell was just waiting on that call from his private investigator to hear anything in regards to Journee. It seemed today might be his lucky day.

Rendell's office phone rang and he answered it while still typing on his laptop. He then stopped typing and devoted his full attention to his private investigator on the phone. "Wait a minute, so you found her? Well, where is she? Is she alright?" Rendell then stood from his chair. He listened to his private investigator and then frowned. He swallowed hard and then nodded while listening. "Yeah, ok…just send the address to my cell and I'll take it from there…thanks." He ended the call and then sighed. It wasn't the call that Rendell was hoping for, but at least his wife was found and that was the most important thing at the moment. Rendell decided to shut down early and call his sister on the way home. He would speak to her about what the private investigator told him.

About an hour later, Rendell walked in the house with Ju; Meela couldn't watch him today, so Ju was in daycare. Rendell got Ju settled in the playroom with juice and a snack; he then waited for Meela and Rydell. Rydell was set to start college in the fall at Baylor University, so he was still at home.

Rendell went in the living room and then sat down in his armchair; not too long after, Rydell walked in and looked at his dad. "Hey, dad; what's going on? You alright?" Rendell looked at him and then shook his head. "Uh, no, I'm not, son; I'm waiting for your aunt so I can speak to both of you together." Rydell nodded and understood since Meela was a very important aspect in the family; she played the mother role to Rydell after his mother died and until Journee came along. Rydell sat down and hoped it wasn't bad news that his dad was going to give the family.

Meela entered the house with her key; she only started using it after Journee disappeared. She hurried to the living room and found Rendell and Rydell sitting with sad looks on their faces. She stopped in her tracks and slowly moved her head from side to side. "Oh no, Ren…what happened? Is Journee alright?" Rendell looked at his sister and then told her to have a seat. She was in panic mode, as well as Rydell. Meela and Journee weren't just sisters-in-law but had become good friends.

Rendell sighed and then shook his own head. "The private investigator found Journee…he found her in Atlanta and with another man. He couldn't say who the other man was but it looked like they were arguing." Rydell and Meela had their mouths open; they looked at each other and then back to Rendell. He sat back against the armchair and then sighed, while Meela was speechless. "Ok, what the…are you serious? There's no way in hell she left you for another guy; he probably kidnapped her or something, I mean…" Rendell angrily interjected. "Fuck all that, Meela!" Rydell jumped when his dad yelled and Meela was still in disbelief.

Rendell stood from the armchair. "I'm going to Atlanta to get my wife back…in fact we're all gonna go get Journee back. If she left me for another man, then I wanna hear it from her mouth." Meela sighed, and then spoke. "Maybe he made a mistake, Ren; Journee wouldn't do this…I'm telling you she wouldn't do this, but yeah, I'm in. I just want you to be calm before we see her." Rydell was on board to do whatever to get Journee back as well. Since it was now decided of what the Murphy family was going to do, Rendell went to get Ju and get him settled. Meela shook her head and then looked at Rydell; they hoped all went well in regards to Journee.

Chapter 6

One week before…

There was a knock on the door and Corrina went to see who it was; she opened the door and nearly lost her breath. She stepped back and then put her hand over her mouth; she removed her hand and then shook her head from side to side. "Jaeda? Oh, my fucking God…where the hell you been?" Corrina lunged forward and the women embraced; they cried together as well. They pulled apart and then Jaeda wiped her face. Corrina pulled her inside the apartment and then closed the door. Jaeda put her hand on her forehead and then shook her head. "Corrina…I tried to call Devonte and his number was disconnected. I woke up in a strange house and found out I was in Texas. I don't know what happened, but all I could think about was Devonte and you. Where is he and what's going on?" Jaeda continued to cry, as Corrina pulled Jaeda to her and hugged her tight. "It's alright, Jaeda…we looked for you after the accident, but we never found you. They said two more years and you'd be declared legally dead. Devonte is gonna have a stroke when he sees you."

Jaeda pulled back from her best friend and then wiped her face again; she was about to speak when she turned her head and did a doubletake. She noticed the calendar on the wall; she then pointed. "What the hell does that say? That can't be right, Corrina…the calendar; what happened to me, Corrina?"

Corrina put her hands on Jaeda's shoulders and looked at her. "Jaeda, they found your car five years ago…but you weren't in it. It was all banged up and we all thought the worst. Nobody could find you and Devonte thought you were dead or kidnapped. Where you been all this time, I mean, what happened to you?" Jaeda shrugged her shoulders; she didn't know and couldn't remember the last five years of her life. "I don't know…the last thing I remember is driving to the bank; the night before, me and Devonte were talking about the sandwich shop. Where is he?" Corrina nodded. Although skeptical, it wasn't her place; she couldn't believe her best friend didn't remember the last five years of her life.

Corrina told Jaeda that she was going to call Devonte and Jaeda nodded; both women went to the living room. Jaeda sat on the couch and then bounced her leg up and down on the floor. She sighed several times and was nervous about seeing Devonte again; she didn't know what he would think or if he would believe her story, something she didn't even believe.

Corrina went to her bedroom where her cell phone was. After a few moments, Corrina returned and joined Jaeda in the living room. "He's on his way…he was at work." Jaeda nodded and then thanked her. Corrina didn't know what else to say since it was clear Jaeda couldn't answer any questions. The women sat there in silence until there was a knock on the door about ten minutes later. Corrina stood from the couch, as well as Jaeda. Jaeda stood there and waited, as Corrina disappeared from of the living room.

When she returned, she had Devonte with her. Devonte stopped in his tracks when he saw his former fiancée; he slowly walked over to her, as Corrina watched. Jaeda slightly smiled; he stopped when he reached her. "Baby…is that really you? Damn…I thought you were, I mean, you're here." Devonte reached forward and grabbed Jaeda, as she sighed in relief. She didn't know what she expected, but to be embraced so lovingly was a good start in her eyes.

Devonte pulled back from Jaeda and looked at her. "Where you been, baby…what happened?" Jaeda looked at Corrina and then back to Devonte; she explained about her last memory and that she couldn't remember the apparent last five years. Devonte was stunned and didn't know if he could believe Jaeda or not but knew one way to get the truth about what was going on. "Ok baby, I'ma take you to the hospital; something must of happened after your accident for you to forget." Jaeda nodded and agreed. He smiled and then looked at Corrina; he thanked her and she nodded. Corrina then watched as Devonte and Jaeda left. Afterwards, Corrina sat down on the couch and sighed.

Chapter 7

Devonte and Jaeda spent about four hours at the hospital. She was examined and the doctors determined that she had amnesia, but they were puzzled. A second opinion had to be given on the first doctor's diagnosis since Jaeda had memory of everything before her accident, but couldn't remember anything after the accident, as if the last five years of her life didn't exist to her anymore. All in all, they diagnosed her with Retrograde Amnesia.

Devonte bid a sigh of relief, that Jaeda was telling him the truth, but was still curious as to how she made it to Texas after her accident; he wondered who was there and what made her go, but Jaeda had no answer for that. Jaeda did agree to therapy to help with her memory loss. After the long grueling exams, Devonte took Jaeda home. He was no longer in the apartment that they had shared together, before she disappeared, but another apartment: a much bigger one.

When they reached the apartment, he told Jaeda to follow him to the living room; she nodded and looked around as she followed him. She realized that his style had changed and it seemed he did as well. Devonte smiled at her and she smiled back; they sat down and looked at each other. Before he spoke, she did. "I know this is probably hard for you…it's hard for me too, but I love you and I wanna try to make up for the last five years with you if I can. I'm just sorry this happened." She sniffed; he reached forward and then wiped the tears from her cheek with his thumb.

Devonte sighed and then looked down; he then looked back up at her again. "Baby, don't worry about that right now; the important thing is that you're home and safe." Jaeda sighed and then nodded. Now that Jaeda was home, she wasn't worried about the last five years of her life; although Devonte assured her that he wasn't either, in the back of his mind, he was. He suggested they go get something to eat and talk; she agreed.

While out, Devonte couldn't hold off on any more questions in regards to the sandwich shop that he and Jaeda started. He decided not to tell her anything, but to show her instead. Devonte parked on the street and Jaeda frowned when she saw the sandwich shop; she jumped out the car and then ran over to the shop, which was now a shell of what the sandwich shop used to be. It was boarded and basically condemned. Jaeda was devastated when she saw it; Devonte walked over to Jaeda and then stopped next to her. She looked at him. "What the hell happened to the shop?"

Devonte sighed and put his hands in his pockets. "With you gone and all of us trying to find you, I needed money that I borrowed from my parents to keep it going. It hit me hard when I couldn't find you; I neglected the shop and it went under a few months after you disappeared. I'm still paying my parents in installments for the money I borrowed from them. I'm working my ass off to pay them back…since they pay my rent for my apartment."

Jaeda stood there with her mouth open. She tried to keep up with everything that he had just told her. "Wow…I don't know what to say; you just let it go like that? I would of kept the shop for you if something happened, especially if I knew it was your dream. I would of knew that you wouldn't want me to lose it. Only after a few months, Devonte? Really?" Devonte frowned and then leaned his head to the side; he was disgusted with her attitude in regards to decisions he had to make in her absence. He angrily spoke. "You were gone for five fucking years and you're mad at me about losing a business that I didn't even want in the first place? What the hell did you want me to do, Jaeda? We were in debt with the damn shop before you took off."

Jaeda shook her head. "I didn't take off…I apparently had an accident and lost my damn memory, but I guess that's irrelevant to you. I can't give you what we lost together, but I got my memory of us back and I'm trying. Now what the hell do you want me to do?" Devonte was about to say something but held his tongue. He didn't want to continue to argue with her; it felt as if it were déjà vu since before she disappeared, they argued about the same thing. "Look baby, it's been a long time and things changed…I changed, but meet me halfway and we can try to make this work again like before."

Jaeda sighed and then nodded in agreeance. He took her hand and then escorted her back to the car; it was imperative that he get back to work. He wanted to take some time off to be with Jaeda after her return but that was impossible. Jaeda understood and for now she would stay home until she was able to find a job. She didn't have a cell phone, money, or her ID when she returned, so she had to apply for another driver's license and social security card.

Chapter 8

Present day…

The Murphy family exited the plane where their rental SUV was waiting. Ju was asleep and Rendell was carrying him to the vehicle on his shoulder. Once in the vehicle they all strapped in and then Rendell drove to the address that the private investigator gave him. Rendell was nervous; it was the longest two weeks of his life without his wife. They rode in the SUV while in silence; it was an eerie silence to Meela. She was in the backseat with Ju and noticed that Rydell kept glancing at his dad off and on. The blank stare on Rendell's face wasn't comforting to any of them and they hoped he remained calm with whatever they found out in regards to Journee.

After about a thirty-minute drive, they reached their destination. Rendell pulled into an apartment complex and parked in a vacant spot. He frowned and then sighed when he saw the complex. Rydell raised an eyebrow and then cleared his throat. It wasn't as if the apartment complex was rundown or anything of that nature, but to Rendell's standards of living, it was several notches below his lifestyle and how they were all used to living.

Rendell shut the engine off and then sat there for what seemed like forever, until Rydell broke the silence. "Dad…we getting out or what?" Rendell sat there for a few more seconds before turning his head to his son. "Yeah…come on; we'll all go." Before Meela could object to that plan, Rendell had already opened the door and got out the SUV. Rydell and Meela followed his lead along with Ju. While Meela held Ju's hand, they all walked through the complex and searched for the correct apartment.

When they reached the apartment, Rendell looked at his son and then turned back to the door; he raised his arm and then knocked on the door. They stood there for a brief moment before the door opened. Rendell sucked in air, as he stood there and stared at his wife. She slightly smiled, as she looked at everyone at the door. "Uh, can I help y'all with something?" Rydell cleared his throat and Rendell frowned. "Say, what? Journee, baby…it's me; why did you leave, I mean, what's going on with you?" Jaeda slightly stepped back with her hand still on the door. "Uh, I think you got the wrong apartment and person…my name's not Journee; I'm sorry…" She was about to close the door when Rendell stopped it with his hand; she opened it all the way again and frowned with his aggressiveness. "Excuse me, but I'm about to call the police if you and your family don't leave." Jaeda was serious.

Rydell put his hand over his face and Meela sighed; Rendell was enraged. "Family! Don't you mean, your family!" Jaeda jumped and Meela looked at her brother; she attempted to calm him down. Rydell looked around and then back at his dad. "Uh dad, maybe we need to go…" Rendell ignored his son and stared at his wife, as she tried to process what he had just said.

Before anything else could be said, Devonte walked from the bedroom and to the front to see what was going on; the yelling made him concerned. Devonte stood next to Jaeda and then looked at Rendell, as he addressed her. "Baby, are you alright?" Rendell shot Devonte a look. "Baby! You really left me for another man!" Devonte looked at Jaeda and she looked right back at him, as he spoke. "What the hell is he talking about? You left me for this dude?" Meela frowned, while Rydell was confused.

Rendell was mad and then pushed his way inside, while almost knocking Devonte to the floor. "I came for my wife and I'm not leaving without her. Journee, baby…we need to talk about this." Devonte was about to lunge at Rendell when Jaeda and Rydell intervened and separated the men. "Dad, come on, chill out." Rendell shook his head, no; he then picked up Ju and held him, as he looked at Jaeda. "Journee…look…" Devonte angrily interjected. "Her name's not Journee, it's Jaeda, and she's my fiancée, so get out the hell out of here." Rendell wasn't trying to hear anything that Devonte was saying, and was now becoming enraged.

Meela saw this trip as a bad move on their part; she thought that maybe Rendell should have come by himself, but then again if he did, then he would end up fighting and getting in trouble.

Jaeda shook her head. "I'm sorry, but he's right…my name's not Journee and I don't know who you are, any of y'all." Rendell shook his head; while he was doing this, Devonte had pulled his cell phone out and called the police, while Rendell was still in disbelief. "What the hell are you talking about? We've been married for four years and we have a son together…Dell, is your stepson. Why are you doing this, Journee?" Jaeda was dumbfounded, as well as Devonte. He ended the call once he finished speaking to the operator; he then walked back over to the group. "A son? You got married to this dude and had a baby, Jaeda?" Devonte was no longer angry anymore, but becoming hurt by his former fiancée's apparent double life. Jaeda vigorously shook her head. "No, Devonte…I don't, I mean, I…" Jaeda couldn't get any more words out. Arguing ensued amongst them and not too long after, the police officers walked up to the door; everyone turned around.

One officer asked what the problem was. Devonte angrily spoke before anyone else could. "I don't have a problem, but this dude and these people barged in my apartment and won't leave." Rendell handed Ju over to Meela and then looked at the officers. "This is my wife and he brainwashed her or something; she went missing two weeks ago from Houston and there's a missing person's report filed on her. Her name is Journee Murphy, and she's my wife." Rendell took his wallet out his pocket and showed one of the officers a picture of the family with Jaeda in it and the copy of the police report he filed.

Devonte wanted this to stop, as well as Jaeda. As the officer looked at the items, Jaeda couldn't take this anymore. "Just, stop!" They all looked at her, even Rendell. Jaeda sighed. "Two weeks ago, I woke up in a strange bed, a strange house, and in a strange city…I couldn't remember how I got there, but I did remember my fiancé Devonte, so I made my way back here to Atlanta. I found out I was in an accident five years ago and had amnesia. I don't remember the last five years at all, so whatever I did or whoever I was with is irrelevant to me now. I'm back home and with the man I love…the man I was engaged to and planned to marry five years ago."

Meela stood there with her mouth open; she and Rydell slowly turned their heads to Rendell. He stepped closer to Jaeda and stared at her. "Amnesia? This can't be real…you're my wife and we have a damn son, Journee. You can't possibly expect me to forget five years of my damn life with you. We can get you some help and get your memories back that you had with me and the rest of us, including your son." The officers stood by and watched; they were confused about what to do with this situation.

Jaeda looked at Devonte and then back to Rendell. "I'm sorry, but I don't remember and I don't wanna remember; this is my life and I belong here." Devonte once again told them to leave. Rydell grabbed his dad's arm, as he continued to stare at his wife. "Dad, come on; let's just go…we gotta go now before they arrest you." Rendell looked at the officers and then at his son;

he nodded and Meela was relieved that her brother complied. Rendell looked at Jaeda one last time before backing away and then turning around to leave. Rydell and Meela looked at Jaeda too and then left with Ju afterwards. The officers asked questions, and Jaeda and Devonte explained the situation again. Afterwards, the officers left.

Chapter 9

Devonte closed the door and then turned around to Jaeda; she thought he was going to say something, but he didn't. Devonte couldn't even look at her right now. Regardless if she had amnesia or not, she started an entire new life and family while gone.

Jaeda stopped him when he was about to walk around her; he stopped and looked at her, as she spoke. "Are you alright?" He frowned and then snatched his arm away from her. "That's not a serious question, is it? You got married and had a baby…you don't remember none of that, but it still happened Jaeda. How the hell am I supposed to feel about that? I don't even know if you coming back was even a good thing anymore; with all this going on, it might of been better if you never got your memory back of us being together."

Jaeda stood there with a saddened look on her face; he shook his head and then went back to the bedroom. Jaeda threw her hands up and then sighed; she didn't know how to make this right. His words to her hurt, but she suspected all of this hurt him as well. With her return, all they were doing was hurting each other.

Jaeda walked to the bedroom and then opened the door to find Devonte lying on the bed with his hands behind his head and his legs crossed at the ankles. She walked over to the bed and then sat down. "I don't know what you want me to say, except I'm sorry for all this. I can't even remember the accident to tell you what happened with that either, but know that I love you and I want you, not him." Jaeda didn't wait for a response; she stood back up from the bed and then left the bedroom. Devonte stared at the ceiling the entire time but turned his head after she left. He wanted to say he was sorry so badly but was too stubborn to let the words out. Neither could replace the last five years of their lives, but once again he was willing to try if possible.

*   *   *

After the Murphy family got back in the SUV; Rendell slammed the door and then sat there. All was quiet, since no one knew what to say. Ju had fallen asleep in the car seat and Meela was thankful for that. Rendell seemed as if he didn't want to leave but knew that he had to.

Meela looked at her brother. "Ren…what do you wanna do now?" He sighed and looked in the rearview mirror at his sister. He started to laugh and Rydell looked at his dad; he thought he was having a nervous breakdown. Rendell stopped laughing and then shook his head. "What do I wanna do? I don't know what the hell to do, Meela; my wife doesn't know me or her son. She basically told me to go fuck myself and that the last five years never happened. With all that, you tell me what to do now." Meela stayed quiet since she didn't have an answer for her brother. Rendell made a sarcastic sound and then started the vehicle; afterwards, he said, nothing, and then drove out the apartment complex.

They decided to get a hotel room for the night and grab something to eat; they would fly back to Houston the next morning. This would give Rendell a chance to decide whether or not he would return to see Jaeda again or take the life he had with her as a loss.

Chapter 10

One month later…

Jaeda had found a job as a cook in a five-star restaurant, but the tension was still there at home between her and Devonte. It was as if they were starting over from scratch with their relationship. Jaeda had been also thinking about the Murphy family; although she had no recollection of them, she was still curious about her married life with Rendell. She often knocked those thoughts out her head and continued to work to keep busy. Devonte also worked to keep busy and make the money that he so desperately needed. In five years, Jaeda returned to the same situation with Devonte, that she was in before she left: a life of debt.

While on her break, Jaeda sat at the bar and ate a sandwich; it reminded her of her sandwich shop. As she sat there and ate, she glanced up and then did a doubletake; Corrina was walking towards her. Jaeda smiled when Corrina reached her; she smiled in return. "Hey, lady…I just came to see how the new job was going." Corrina sat down on the stool next to Jaeda and looked at her.

Jaeda slightly laughed and then nodded. "Well, thanks and the job is good; I'm back doing what I love…even if it's not in my own business." Jaeda looked at her drink and then sighed. Corrina frowned and then leaned her head to the side. "So, you still mad about the sandwich shop?" Jaeda looked up at Corrina and then shook her head. "No, it's not that…I uh, been thinking about going to see that guy, Rendell…Rendell Murphy; you remember what I told you happened that day, right? Well, I still don't remember, but I'm just curious about that family."

Corrina sighed and didn't think that was a good idea. "Maybe you should just leave it alone, Jaeda; you said you had your life back and this was what you wanted…that Devonte was what you wanted, so leave pandora's box closed." Jaeda listened to Corrina but couldn't let this go; it was the unknown that bothered her. The fact that she had a son was another reason she needed to speak to Rendell. For the meantime she would leave it alone, but when possible, she planned to fly to Houston and see Rendell. Jaeda told Corrina that she had to get back to work and Corrina understood. Corrina stood from the stool and then hugged Jaeda, goodbye.

Afterwards, Corrina left and Jaeda sighed. Before she could finish her sandwich, her co-worker and now friend, Daniel, walked over to her. "Hey, are you alright?" Jaeda looked at him and then nodded. "Uh, yeah…you remember what I told you about my amnesia, right?" Daniel nodded, as he sat down on the stool that Corrina was previously sitting on. Jaeda looked at her sandwich and then back to Daniel. "Ok, well…I'm thinking about going to Houston to see the Murphy family. I told Corrina and she didn't think it was a good idea. What do you think?" Daniel sighed and then slightly nodded his head; he understood why Jaeda needed to see the Murphy family, even if Corrina didn't. "Well, I think if it'll help you get answers or whatever, then you should do it. I mean, you spent five years with this guy and had a kid, so maybe that's worth looking into, even if it's to get closure."

Jaeda slightly smiled, as he frowned. "What?" Jaeda shook her head. "Corrina's been my friend since forever, but she acted like I was making a mistake if I went to Houston. I hadn't known you that long, but it's like we been friends for years. Thanks for having my back." Daniel smiled. "Anytime, Jaeda…you know if you ever need anything, then all you have to do is ask. And that friend, Corrina…maybe you should watch out for her; something don't seem right about her, but that's just the vibe I get from her." Jaeda slightly frowned. "What vibe? You don't really know her."

Daniel sighed; he looked around and then back to Jaeda, before he spoke again. "Look, Jaeda…I know she was your best friend before your accident, but it's not five years ago anymore…but five years later. She's still single and from what you said, been hanging around with your fiancé the whole time you were gone. So…" Jaeda interjected. "So, what? This was hard for Devonte and he needed somebody there for him, after

I went missing, so…" She stopped talking and Daniel sighed; he assumed Jaeda caught the hint of where he was going with his words.

Jaeda turned her head to the side and understood where Daniel was coming from in regards to Corrina; she didn't want to admit it, but Jaeda also felt that something wasn't right with Corrina, ever since she returned to Devonte. For now, Jaeda was going to let that go.

Jaeda looked back at Daniel and smiled. "Uh, we need to get back to work. Daniel nodded. She cleaned up her area and then they got off the stools; they hugged before they got back to work.

Chapter 11

Back in Houston, Rendell was at work and in the middle of a conference. He was frustrated and it could be seen by his staff. Working to stay sane hadn't been easy for him since Journee left and then refused to return. He became agitated during the meeting and told everyone to get out of his office. Afterwards, he sat down behind his desk and rubbed his hands down his face. He removed his hands and then rocked back and forth in his chair.

While thinking, there was a knock at his office door; he wasn't in the mood to see anyone, but the knocks continued. He had enough and yelled for whoever it was to come in. The door opened and Meela walked in; Rendell rolled his eyes, as she closed the door behind her. She shook her head, as she walked over to her brother's desk. She stopped and then sat down in the chair across from his desk. Meela said nothing but instead stared at her brother. He frowned and then once again had enough. "What, Meela?" She sighed and then shrugged her shoulders. "Well, one of your paralegals called me for an intervention of your attitude and hostility." Rendell once again frowned and then slightly nodded. "Alright, well, after I fire the snitch, then we should be good. I don't have an attitude and I damn sure don't need an intervention…bye, Meela."

Rendell was about to stand from his chair, when Meela stopped him. "You gotta find a way to cope with this." Rendell slowly sat back down in his chair and then turned his head to the side; he turned back to his sister and then slightly laughed. "Cope with this? How the hell am I supposed to cope with this, Meela? My wife left me and the boys; not to mention that she doesn't remember us any damn way. We were in love and had the perfect life, and in a split second it was over. I can't deal with losing Journee, not this way…" Rendell was highly upset.

Meela sighed. She wished she could help her brother through this; she not only lost a sister-in-law, but she also lost a friend. Regardless, the most important thing out of all of this was that Journee was still the mother of Ju and he needed his mother, as much as he needed his father. "Ok look, I say talk to her and remind her that she has a son; that's one way to maybe get her mind right." Rendell frowned at his sister's ridiculous plan. "You can't be serious; if she can't remember her own child then…you know what, just forget about this. I'm gonna get over this and her, so I'm fine. No need for you to stop by my job anymore either." Meela sighed and then nodded. She realized that nothing she could say would help her brother or the situation. She stood from the chair and then looked at her brother. "Alright, Ren…you got it all figured out, so I'll drop this. I'll see you later and Dell is picking up Ju from daycare."

Rendell nodded and then watched, as Meela turned around to leave his office. After she was gone, Rendell sat back against his chair and then thought about what his sister said. He also thought about Journee again, but knew he needed to stop before he completely lost his mind. Rendell decided to continue to try to get her out of his head, by once again attempting to work.

Chapter 12

Back in Atlanta, it was a week later and Devonte had gotten off from work early; he responded to a text message that was sent to him. When he reached his apartment, he saw that Corrina was waiting outside the door. Devonte slowed down his pace and then stopped when he reached Corrina; he looked at her and then unlocked the door. After both went inside, he closed the door behind them and then offered her a drink. Corrina declined, as he knew she would. He also knew why she was there and what she wanted. He threw his keys on the end table in the living room and then sat down on the couch; she followed his lead and then crossed her legs.

Devonte sat there and waited for her to say something. "Alright, Corrina…let me have it." She frowned and then sarcastically laughed. "I been letting you have it for seven years, Devonte. What's going on? Did you forget about me now that Jaeda is back?" Devonte sighed and then stood from the couch. "What do you want me to do? I didn't know this was gonna happen…regardless, we can't be together right now. I can't tell my fiancée that I was fucking with her best friend before and after she disappeared; I don't wanna hurt her feelings."

Corrina frowned and then stood from the couch. She stared at Devonte with anger and hurt. "Your fiancée? She hadn't been your damn fiancée in five fucking years, Devonte. We were about to move in together before she came back…you told me you loved me. I was your sideline before and after you proposed to her. Now you making me your side bitch again?" Devonte was about to speak, when she did again. "We're still fucking each other on your lunch breaks since she got back too, but you don't wanna hurt her feelings?" Devonte sucked his teeth and was about to speak, but Corrina continued on her rant. "Just forget about it…I'm not doing this with you no more; she had a happy life with another man, got married, and had a baby, but you still thinking about her damn wants and needs? You and Jaeda can do whatever."

Corrina was about to walk away and leave, when he grabbed her arm to stop her. Devonte pulled her to him and then put his arms around her waist. "Baby, I'm sorry…I'm not dismissing you or what we got going, but the timing was never right for me and you. This shit is hard, so give me some time to figure this out…please, I love you and I still need you."

Devonte's lies came more smoother and easier with each passing day, since he started his affair with Corrina. She believed any and everything he said to her, in regards to why they could never be together the right way, and why he had to stay with Jaeda, even before her disappearance. Devonte never had any intention of making Corrina his main woman for several reasons. His parents didn't like Jaeda, but they would permanently disown him if he ever brought Corrina to their doorstep. As far as Devonte was concerned, Corrina was only good for one thing, and could never be wife material. Her role, unbeknownst to her, in his life, was to be his sideline.

Corrina looked to the side and then back to Devonte; she nodded her head and he sighed in relief. He slightly jerked his head to the side and licked his lips; she slightly laughed and then nodded again. He stepped back from her and then took her hand. Devonte then led Corrina to the bedroom; he closed the door behind them.

Chapter 13

Jaeda left work early since she wasn't feeling well; she entered the apartment and then threw her purse and keys on the end table. She noticed that Devonte's keys were also on the end table. She didn't think he would be home early from work so she didn't notice that his truck was parked outside.

Jaeda looked around and was about to call out for Devonte when she heard something. She frowned, as she started to slowly walk down the hall and towards the bedroom. When she reached the bedroom door, she heard noises coming from the other side. Jaeda put her ear to the door and after a few seconds she quickly removed it. Although hesitant, Jaeda put her hand out and slowly turned the knob to the bedroom door; she took a deep breath and then slowly opened it.

Jaeda was horrified when she saw and heard Devonte; he was in between Corrina's legs. He had one hand on the headboard, as Corrina was licking his neck. Jaeda was speechless; she slowly closed the bedroom door and then walked back towards the living room. She looked around and then put her hand over her mouth, as she silently cried to herself. She couldn't believe this was happening. It did make sense to her now about Devonte's mood towards her lately, as well as Corrina. Daniel's concerns and hers, were now confirmed.

Regardless of what she suspected or felt, thinking and knowing, were two different things. Jaeda was devastated and didn't know what to do now. She did know that she needed to get out of there. She grabbed her purse and keys and then left the apartment. She got back in her car and then left the apartment complex.

After driving around for what seemed like forever, Jaeda parked in a vacant lot and then called Devonte. Because some time had passed, she assumed that he and Corrina would be finished. When he answered, she was unsure of what to say and how to act. "Uh hey, you at work?" She nodded after he said, he was. Devonte actually was back at work now; he returned to work after he and Corrina were finished. She sighed and then listened to him. She then shook her head. "I'm on my way home…I don't feel good, so I'm headed there now."

Jaeda heard the noise in the background indicating that he was at work. "Yeah ok, well, I love you…bye." She ended the call and then looked at the phone. She understood now where Devonte's comment about her not returning came from. Jaeda left the parking lot and then headed back home, but she wasn't staying for long. She planned to pack a small bag and leave again for Houston. She thought that this was the best time to know about her old life that she couldn't remember.

Chapter 14

It was later that night in Houston, when Rendell's doorbell rang; Ju was asleep already and Rydell was out for the evening. Rendell wasn't expecting anyone but walked out his living room anyway to see who was at his door. When he reached the door, he looked through the peephole. A frown came upon his face; he definitely wasn't expecting who was on the other side of the door. He hesitated for a moment and then opened the door; he came face to face with Jaeda.

Rendell stared at her, before he spoke. "Is there something I can help you with?" Jaeda clutched her handbag and looked down; she then looked back up at Rendell. She took a chance and decided to take the first flight from Atlanta to Houston. "Uh yeah, Mr. Murphy…I was wondering if we could talk." Rendell slightly laughed, but in a sarcastic manner. "Mr. Murphy? Yeah ok, come in." Jaeda nodded and then walked inside after he stepped to the side. He closed the door behind her and then she followed him to the living room. After they sat down, Rendell waited for her to say something. Jaeda cleared her throat and then sighed. "How did we meet…I mean, what was our life like?" He frowned.

Rendell was dumbfounded that she had the audacity to come to his home after what happened at hers the previous month, but he also remembered what his sister said. He did need to move on and if it took him answering her questions to accomplish that, then he would do it. He sat back against the couch and continued to stare at her, as she waited. "We met at a shelter, five years ago; I was there to talk to the manager about a case and you were volunteering. It was love at first sight for me…I asked you out and we dated for about six months before I proposed; six months after that, we were married. A year later, we had our son Rendell Jr., but everyone calls him Ju. I have a son from a previous relationship named Rydell, but everyone calls him Dell; he graduated from high school last month."

Jaeda nodded and then sat closer to the edge of the couch. Although she couldn't remember their encounter, she needed to know all of this. "Uh yeah, can I get a drink? Vodka, Crown, or something strong?" He raised an eyebrow and then nodded. He got up and then went to the bar to make her something to drink, as she sat there and waited. When he finished, he walked back over to her and then handed her the glass; he then put his hands in his pockets, as he stood there and stared at her. She thanked him and almost swallowed it all down in the first gulp.

Rendell slightly shook his head. "You never used to drink when we were together…" She looked up at him after he spoke. "Oh, yeah? Well, I don't know, but I'm definitely a drinker." She slightly laughed, while his facial expression remained the same. Before she could speak again, he did. "Ok look, this is probably easy for you since you don't remember me or your family, but it's not for me. I answered enough questions and I can't do this with you anymore. I remember our life from the time we met and became a family. I have to act like the last five years didn't exist and you being here is not making this any better. I need to move on, so you can't come back here again." Rendell was serious and then told her to leave.

Jaeda looked up at him and then stood from the couch; she bent down to set her glass on the coffee table and then picked up her handbag. She said nothing, as she walked around Rendell and then headed to the front; he followed her. When she reached the front door, she stopped and then turned around. "What about your son…well, our son?" Rendell stood there and stared at her for a few seconds before responding. "Have a good life, Journee…" She sighed and then became angry. "It's Jaeda…and about that good life…I don't see how that's gonna happen. None of this is easy for me either; I been apologizing to everybody since I got my memory back. Once again, I'm sorry…I'm fucking sorry I hurt you and Devonte, but what do y'all want me to do? I didn't mean for this to happen, I mean…I was in an accident, so how the hell are y'all pissed off at me for having amnesia?"

Jaeda stopped and then put her hand up; she shook her head, as she looked down and thought about Devonte and her best friend being together. Jaeda looked back up with watery eyes this time. Rendell's facial expression changed; he was no longer angry, but sympathetic. Before he could speak, she did again. "Don't...the only thing I learned from all this is that you can't turn back time...I don't belong in my old memories anymore and I don't belong in my new ones. So, you have a good fucking life...Mr. Murphy."

Jaeda was about to open the front door, when Rendell went forward and then grabbed her arm; he jerked her around and stared at her, as neither said nothing. He then pulled Jaeda to him and kissed her; she opened her mouth and their tongues wrestled with each other. Jaeda dropped her handbag by the front door and they fully embraced each other. He pushed her back against the front door and they continued to kiss vigorously. Even though Jaeda didn't remember the instant attraction between her and Rendell, he did. He also remembered their love making.

Rendell slightly pulled back from Jaeda and then bit his bottom lip, as he stared at her. She cleared her throat and although this seemed wrong to her, she questioned whether it was really wrong since Devonte was cheating on her anyway with Corrina. She opened her mouth to speak and he put his finger to her lips to silence her. He removed his finger and then pulled Jaeda away from the front door; he picked her up and then walked away from the front while carrying her. He made his way upstairs and to the bedroom to make love to his wife again.

Chapter 15

The next morning, Rendell was in the kitchen and feeding Ju, breakfast. Rydell yawned on his way into the kitchen. Rendell nodded. "Good morning, son…" Rydell gave his dad a head nod and then sat down at the table. Rendell heard the front door and knew that was Meela, since she had been coming over for breakfast every Saturday morning.

As Meela made it to the kitchen, Jaeda made her way to the kitchen from the other entrance. Meela stopped in her tracks and Rydell did a doubletake; he started to choke on his food. Rendell slightly smiled at Jaeda and she cleared her throat at everyone. "Uh, good morning…Rendell, I'm about to head out. Can I meet him?" Rendell nodded, while Rydell and Meela were still speechless.

Jaeda and Rendell walked over to Ju and then stopped. Before Rendell could say anything, Ju finally looked up from his food and smiled. "Mommy!" Ju jumped up from his chair and Jaeda slightly stepped back from the toddler, but then stopped to embrace his hug. She and Devonte didn't want children, so she was surprised to know that while she had amnesia, she had a son with Rendell.

As they hugged, Meela shot her brother a look, as Rydell watched the awkward interaction between mother and son. Jaeda pulled back from Ju and then smiled at him. "Uh, hey, Ju…I need to go, but I hope to see you again soon." Ju frowned and then started to cry, as Jaeda backed away from him; she looked at Rendell and then quickly made her way out the kitchen to leave. Ju cried harder for his mama and Rendell sighed; Meela went to him and comforted the toddler. She looked at her brother. "What the hell was that? I mean, how…what…?" Rydell laughed at his aunt and Rendell rolled his eyes. Ju stopped crying and Meela was thankful for that.

Rendell shook his head. "Not today, Meela…" He picked up Ju to make sure he was alright; he then set him back down and watched the toddler run out the kitchen. Meela threw her hands up. "Not today? What was Journee doing here?" Rendell decided to indulge his sister so she would leave him alone. "She came over last night to talk, and on her way out…just never mind how it started but it happened. It's not a big deal anyway; I made love to my wife last night." Rydell and Meela frowned, but for different reasons. "That's disgusting, dad…" Rendell leaned his head to the side, as he looked at his son. "Making love to my wife is disgusting?"

Rydell slightly laughed. "You making love to anybody is disgusting, so I'm not biased. I don't wanna hear that while I'm eating my breakfast." Meela rolled her eyes and Rendell told his son to shut up; he then looked back at his sister. He said, he would talk to her in the living room in private. She nodded and then followed her brother.

When they reached the living room, they stopped and then looked at each other. "I know what we talked about and believe me, I wasn't expecting this to happen, but she is still my wife and I think we both needed this." Meela threw her hands up and then shook her head. "Come on, Ren…did you see how she was with Ju? She still don't remember any of us. You fucking her is not gonna make this easier. She's not Journee anymore…she's not your wife anymore, so for yourself and the boys you need to move on; get the divorce too. You're still in love with her and she feels nothing for you, so you're just gonna hurt yourself."

Rendell sighed and then nodded. "I get what you're saying, but don't worry, Meela…it was a one-time thing and it won't happen again." Meela was skeptical of her brother's answer, but she accepted it. Sometimes she felt as if she were the older sibling, but both had looked out for each other since they were children; after their parents died.

Meela nodded. "Alright, Ren…well, I'ma head back in the kitchen and eat; I don't work tonight if you need me to watch Ju for something." He nodded and then watched his sister walk away. Rendell rubbed his hands down his face and then sighed; he hoped it was just a one-time thing with Jaeda.

After breakfast, Meela left and Rydell was about to go upstairs and get ready for the day when Rendell stopped his son. Rydell turned to his dad. "What's going on, dad?" Rendell looked down and then back up again at his son. "Look, what happened last night with me and your mama…" Rydell put his hand up to stop his dad. "No, dad…she's not my mama for one, and for two, it's none of my business, but I hope you know what you doing. I'll do anything for you and Ju, so this new woman, Jaeda, that was in your bed last night, better not do anything to hurt you or my little brother." Rendell looked to the side and then back to his son; he nodded. He wanted to say more but speaking to his son about this was a lost cause with the way Rydell was feeling about all of this. Rendell decided to leave it alone. Rydell pat his dad on the back and said he would see him later. Rendell sighed and then went to get Ju; he was going to get him ready and then take him to the park.

Chapter 16

Jaeda was in her hotel room and sitting on the bed with her hands together; she was thinking about the night before. She was also thinking about Devonte and Corrina. She now knew that Devonte meant what he said about her not getting her memory back; she also understood why now. Jaeda was confused about what she was supposed to do now and which way to go. She didn't belong to anyone anymore and was actually a rock stuck in between a hard place; stuck in between two worlds that she didn't belong in anymore. What she experienced last sighnt with Rendell felt right; it felt like love, like what she used to have with Devonte before her accident. Because of Devonte's distance and anger towards her now, she wasn't feeling the love that they once had for each other. The problem was, she knew Devonte, but she didn't know Rendell. Their sexual encounter the previous night also felt like a one-night stand.

Jaeda's cell phone rang and she took it from her hip; she saw it was Devonte. She sighed, but still didn't answer his call. She didn't tell him she was going to Houston to see Rendell; she didn't want him to know where she was. Her cell phone eventually stopped ringing and she was thankful. She wanted to confront Devonte for lying to her but changed her mind. Her absence is what made him fall in love with her best friend.

Jaeda was unaware of Devonte and Corrina's motive for not telling her about them, but she suspected it had to do with her abrupt return. She was also unaware that they had been having an affair before and after he proposed to her. Jaeda rubbed her hands down her face and then looked around the hotel room; she got up and then went to take a shower before she caught her return flight back to Atlanta.

It was early the next morning and Jaeda returned home with her bag; she walked through the front door while dead tired. She closed the door behind her and then dropped her bag; she sighed and then walked to the living room where Devonte was. He was sitting on the couch when she entered the living room and then looked up. He stood from the couch and then went over to Jaeda, as she stood there. "Baby, where the hell you been? You take off and don't tell me; you don't answer none of my damn calls either. I thought you pulled another disappearance like you did five years ago."

Jaeda stared at Devonte and then shook her head. He was lying to her with a straight face and insulting her at the same time. Jaeda swallowed hard before she spoke. "Sorry…I just needed some time to myself. You should of called Corrina if you were bored or lonely." She had no expression on her face; she walked around Devonte and then to the bedroom. He frowned, as he watched her and wondered what she meant by that statement. He didn't think for a second that she knew about him and Corrina, so it didn't cross his mind. He decided to leave her alone for a while and let her calm down.

Chapter 17

A week went by and Jaeda was back to her reality; not only was she not happy, but she was undecided about her life anymore with Devonte, who she knew was still cheating on her with Corrina: the sideline. Jaeda still hadn't confronted him and she didn't think she would. At this point, whether she wanted to admit it or not, Devonte was all she had. Even though it was apparent to her that she wasn't the love of Devonte's life anymore, leaving him would mean she had no one. She decided to ride this out and see if maybe something changed once they became reacquainted with each other again, even while he continued to cheat on her.

Jaeda was at work and in the kitchen; her manager came to the back to let her know that someone was there to see her. Jaeda stopped what she was doing and wiped her hands on a towel before exiting the kitchen. When she got closer to the front, she stopped when she saw Rendell standing by the bar. Jaeda looked down at herself; she wiped her hands on her apron and then looked around. She looked a mess in her eyes with grease still on her hands and sauce spilled on her shoes. Before she could retreat back to the kitchen to clean herself up, Rendell turned around and spotted Jaeda. He nodded to her and slightly smiled. Jaeda slightly smiled back and then walked over to him.

When she reached him, she looked down at herself again and then back up again at him. He glanced at her as well and then put his hands in his pockets. He was in work attire with his three-piece suit on. Jaeda slightly nodded. "Uh hey, Mr.... I mean, Rendell. What are you doing here?" He asked if they could have a seat; she nodded and then they sat at the bar. She went ahead and decided to take her break. She took her cigarettes out her apron pocket and then lit one, as he raised an eyebrow. "You smoke too? I can tell the difference between Jaeda and Journee clearly, but uh, I was in town for a case and I thought I'd look you up to see how you were doing. This is a nice restaurant…what do you do here?"

Jaeda was surprised to see Rendell, but it did make her day that he was here. She looked around and then back to him. "I'm a chef…I took culinary classes after high school. I had a sandwich shop before I left too, but Devonte let it foreclose or whatever. Anyway, I love to cook and my dream was to have my own restaurant one day." Rendell nodded, as he listened; she cleared her throat. She knew that he probably wanted to speak about what happened between them; she wanted to as well.

Rendell sighed. "Well, that's something…a restaurant; I didn't know you had dreams of that nature. It makes sense…when were together, you were one hell of a cook, but you couldn't tell me who taught you how to cook. You always said you couldn't remember…um, about that night…" Jaeda stopped him before he went any further. "I don't wanna talk about it; I guess I just wanted to see what it was like to be with you. Devonte was my first and only…besides you, but I only remember him." Rendell sighed; that wasn't the response he hoped for when bringing this topic up. He wondered if his words to her before she was about to leave his home that night, was the reason for her words to him now. Regardless, he had to let this go with Jaeda before he made himself crazy.

Rendell cleared his throat and then stood from the stool, before he looked at her again. "I understand, Journee, I mean, Jaeda; I guess that night was closure for both of us, but about Ju…" Jaeda stopped him and then put out her cigarette. "Yeah, about him. I probably should of told you that me and Devonte never wanted kids; I never wanted kids. I wanted to focus on making my dream happen…I'm five years behind now, but I'm working on it. I guess what I'm trying to say is that I don't have a motherly bone in my body. That kid needs somebody that's not me…I'm sorry."

Rendell was outdone; he frowned with her entire statement. This wasn't the woman he knew and was starting to believe now that it was a good thing she left and went back to the life she remembered. The woman he loved and married, loved children and embraced her stepson; he was looking and speaking to a stranger now. Rendell spoke, while irritated. "Ok, Jaeda…well, I guess there's nothing more for us to talk about. You take care and try to have that good life that's most important to you." He didn't give her a chance to respond. He turned and then walked away from Jaeda; she watched him leave the restaurant and then sighed. Jaeda got up from the stool and then went back to work.

Chapter 18

Jaeda got off from work early and didn't call Devonte to tell him; she knew he was off today, so she wanted to see if he was up to no good again with Corrina. It bothered her, but she placed the blame for this on herself. If she hadn't left in the first place, then her fiancé wouldn't have fallen in love with her best friend. It wasn't just that, but Jaeda felt getting her memory back had turned everyone's lives upside down, and not just her own. She now thought that it was a curse instead of a blessing.

After Jaeda arrived at the apartment complex, she parked and then sighed when she saw Corrina's car parked next to Devonte's vehicle. She shook her head and then got out of her car; she walked with her bag to Devonte's apartment. She was reluctant to go inside since she didn't want to encounter Devonte and Corrina in a compromising position, but realized that wouldn't happen this time, since she heard arguing coming from the other side of the door.

Jaeda unlocked the door and then entered. She continued to hear the arguing, but instead of interrupting them, she decided to listen.

Corrina had come over Devonte's apartment because she knew that he was off and Jaeda was at work. What started as a pleasurable visit turned ugly when Corrina brought up Jaeda again.

Corrina had her arms crossed, as she paced the floor. Devonte grabbed Corrina and stopped her. "What the fuck is wrong with you? How many damn times do we gotta argue about the same shit? She's working now, so I'ma guilt her into paying back my parents, the money we lost gambling. I told her I borrowed the money to keep that dumbass sandwich shop open." Corrina sighed and then slightly pushed Devonte back; he frowned, as she yelled. "Fuck that damn sandwich shop and the money you lost! You been stringing me along all these fucking years! You told me before she disappeared that you were gonna end it with her! Seven fucking years with you and we gotta hide our relationship again!?" Devonte tried to calm her down. She wiped her eyes and then put both her hands up to him; she didn't want him to touch her.

Devonte sucked his teeth. "Baby, come on…I told you what the deal is. Me and Jaeda don't even have sex and I hadn't touched her since she came back. I love you and I swear after I get her to pay all that money back then I'ma drop her. Me and you are gonna get married…soon, baby." Corrina sighed and once again, believed the lies that came out of Devonte's mouth, due to how much she loved him.

Before another word could be said, Jaeda came from around the corner. Corrina and Devonte turned their heads in unison. He had his hands on Corrina's cheek, so he abruptly removed them and then smiled at Jaeda. "Baby, what are you doing home so early?" He looked at Corrina and then back to Jaeda. Jaeda stared at Corrina; she turned her face away and then cleared her throat. Jaeda then turned her head to Devonte. "I wasn't feeling good, so I came home early; was I interrupting something? Are you alright, Corrina?"

Corrina turned her head back to Jaeda and then nodded her head, yes; before she could say anything, Devonte spoke for her. "Uh baby, she's upset about some dude that played her, so she came over to talk to me since you were at work. She's good now…and was about to leave before you came in." Corrina shot Devonte a look and then grit her teeth; she slightly smiled and then looked at Jaeda. "Yeah girl, you know these retarded men out there; you were gone, but I was with somebody for a few years until I found out I'm nothing to him but a sidepiece. It hurts, but I'ma be alright…I'll see y'all later."

Corrina grabbed her keys and then glanced at Devonte before walking away. He sighed, since he knew Corrina was speaking about him. Jaeda knew who Corrina was speaking about as well; she heard everything and wanted to cry. It finally clicked in Jaeda's head that her fiancé and best friend were having an affair way before she had her accident.

After Corrina left, Devonte walked over to Jaeda; he took her hands in his. "You want me to get you some orange juice or something? Maybe some soup?" Jaeda swallowed hard and then took her hands away from him; she ignored his question and then walked around him to go to the bedroom. Jaeda wanted nothing more than to get out of his apartment and leave.

Devonte followed her to the bedroom, since she was acting strange. When he walked in the bedroom, he saw Jaeda scrambling around the room and throwing her things on the bed to pack. Devonte raised an eyebrow. "What are you doing? You going somewhere?" Jaeda turned around and looked at him. "I'm leaving…I was gonna tell you sooner, but what the hell…it's not like it matters. I found my own place. This right here is not working for me anymore; we're two different people and I feel like I'm holding you back from something greater." He frowned and then grabbed her arm when she tried to continue packing; he tightened his grip on her and she slightly winced, as she stared at him.

Devonte's entire demeanor and tone changed after hearing all that. "You can't leave…what about the money you owe my parents? I borrowed from them to save your shop after you disappeared, and you do me like this!" She snatched her arm from Devonte and saw the look in his eyes; she realized that something else was going on. She already knew he was lying about the money and that he didn't borrow it from his parents for the sandwich shop, but for a gambling debt.

Jaeda turned her head to the side and then back to him. "I'm leaving, Devonte…" He stepped back from her and then left the bedroom; he paced the floor in the living room and then stopped when Jaeda walked out the bedroom with her bags. She wasn't going to speak to Devonte again, but just walk past him to leave. He made one final attempt to get Jaeda to stay. "Please, baby…I'm sorry for blowing up on you, but I can't lose you; just stay and we can talk about it." She shook her head, no, and then continued to walk away so she could leave.

Devonte heard the front door slam shut. He cursed to himself and then took his cell phone out his pocket. Devonte dialed a number and then waited for someone to answer; he then started to speak when someone did. "Hey…you gotta finish this shit and I mean now; she just left, so clean up your mistake from five years ago, so I can get my damn money." Devonte listened and then nodded on his end; he then said, okay, and ended the call. He rubbed his hand down his face and then went to grab a beer from the refrigerator.

Chapter 19

Jaeda got in her car after she loaded it with her bags; she left the apartment complex afterwards. She didn't know where she was going and lied to Devonte about having her own place now. She just had to get out of there and away from him. She sensed something wasn't right when she saw the look in his eyes and knew she was doing the right thing. Jaeda also couldn't take all the lies straight to her face from him and her former best friend.

Jaeda drove around for what seemed like forever; she didn't have much money and didn't think she could afford a hotel for multiple days. She didn't have a backup plan either and it scared her. Jaeda decided to stop and get something to eat at a fast-food place. After she stopped and parked, she sat there and stared out into space; she was still in disbelief of her life.

Jaeda got out her car and then walked towards the fast-food place, when someone stopped her; she turned to the stranger, and the unknown person spoke. "Hey, Jaeda, it's me Camille...it's been a while since I seen you." Jaeda slightly smiled and then nodded. "Yeah, sure...how's it going?" Camille nodded and then looked around; she cleared her throat and then stepped closer to Jaeda. She whispered. "Turn around and get the hell back out of town, girl..." Jaeda frowned. Camille stepped back and then walked away from Jaeda. She turned around and stared at Camille, as she got in her car and then drove away. Jaeda was confused as to what was going on; she brushed it off and then continued to walk towards the fast-food place. She stopped and then frowned again.

Jaeda had a feeling of familiarity and fear at the same time; she looked at the entrance of the fast-food restaurant and then decided not to go inside. She instead turned around and started to head back to her car. As she did this, a man walked out the restaurant and then spotted Jaeda; he started to walk towards her. He looked around and then jogged towards Jaeda's vehicle; she had already gotten inside and was in the process of starting her car.

As he became closer, he pulled a gun from under his shirt. Jaeda slightly turned her head and then did a doubletake; she started to panic and then abruptly reversed her car. The guy raised his arm and before he could shoot, she put the car in drive and accelerated towards him. He shot and hit her windshield before jumping out the way. She dodged the bullet into her now shattered windshield and then drove straight out the parking lot; Jaeda hit another vehicle and the curb on her way out. She was breathing hard and looking in her rearview mirror, as she drove away. She was confused as to what was happening and who the guy was that was shooting at her.

Jaeda looked through her rearview mirror again and squint her eyes; she saw Camille following her. All of a sudden, Camille sped up, swerved around Jaeda's car aggressively, and then started to honk. Jaeda slammed on her brakes in the middle of the road and then watched as Camille went past her. Camille also slammed on her brakes and then reversed to go back towards Jaeda's car. When she reached her, Jaeda got out her car and then went over to Camille. She banged on the window. "Get the fuck out!" Camille let her window down. "Shut up and get in!" Jaeda was hesitant, but then cursed to herself and nodded. She ran around Camille's car and then got in on the passenger side; Camille quickly drove off, as Jaeda looked behind her. She turned back around to look at Camille. "What the fuck is going on? Who the hell are you and who was that guy that apparently tried to kill me?"

Camille raised an eyebrow and looked from the road to Jaeda; she then looked back at the road and drove to her destination.

Chapter 20

Camille parked in the back of the alley and then sighed. Camille shook her head at Jaeda. "What's wrong with you? Why the hell did you come back? Are you fucking crazy?" Jaeda frowned with the questions and was confused at the same time. "I remembered…that's why I came back…" Camille leaned her head to the side, as she stared at Jaeda. "You remembered, what? What are you talking about?" Jaeda opened her mouth to speak and then closed it; she looked around and then back to Camille. "I uh, remembered my life with Devonte…I was in a car accident and had amnesia five years ago; I woke up in another state and had a family. I don't remember the family I was with, but I remembered my life before the accident, so I came back. I don't know what's going on."

Camille sighed. "Ok, I don't know nothing about your second life, but you don't remember everything…if you remembered then you wouldn't of came back. You got in that car accident because Devonte had somebody chasing you." Jaeda looked down and then back up again at Camille; she didn't remember any of that and questioned whether she should believe or trust Camille. "How the hell do you know all this? How do I know that you're telling me the truth now and not one of them guys that tried to kill me?"

Camille turned her head to the side and then back to Jaeda. "I'm Devonte's sister…I used to help him run dope out that sandwich shop y'all had. You sure you don't remember nothing?" Jaeda was speechless and had no recollection of anything that Camille was talking about. Before she could say anything, Camille spoke again. "You gotta remember, Jaeda…think hard and remember." Jaeda slowly nodded her head and then thought as hard as she could. She thought about the guy that she saw shoot at her; she slightly scrunched her face and then remembered where she saw him before. "That guy at the sandwich shop that day…he said, he was interested in investing in the shop; Devonte came in and I left him with the guy to talk. I went back to work, but that guy was the one that shot at me. I remember leaving for the bank the next morning, but I never made it…that's all I remember."

Camille nodded her head, as she listened but had her own words to add to the story. "Devonte fucked up and gambled away money that wasn't his, so he took out a life insurance policy on you. He was gonna get you killed, collect, and then use the money to pay back a guy named, Stone. I helped you get out that day, Jaeda…I was an informant and I hooked you up with a guy from the FBI to get you out of town. Wherever you came from, you gotta go back and stay gone this time or you're gonna end up dead."

Jaeda was speechless, but still couldn't understand why she didn't remember any of that. "I don't think you understand…I can't go back where I came from; I don't even remember who those people were and they were supposedly my family for the past five years. I don't have any money, or family, or any place to go. What the hell am I gonna do, Camille?" Camille told Jaeda to calm down and that she would take her back to her home for the meantime. Once again Camille was going to help Jaeda get out of town.

Chapter 21

The weekend went by fast for the Murphy household and it was back to business for Rendell. Rydell started a summer job to make money for when he went off to college; Rendell didn't want his son to work while in school, so he could stay focused on his studies.

While Rendell was in his office and in the middle of a conference, his secretary buzzed his phone. Rendell stopped the meeting and answered. "Mr. Murphy, an FBI agent is here to speak to you." Rendell frowned and then looked at his colleagues; he told his secretary to let the agent in and then addressed the others. He ended the conference early As the men were getting up from the chairs, the office door opened and the secretary walked in with the FBI agent.

The men glanced at the man on their way out of the office; the secretary closed the door on her way out, as the FBI agent stood there at the door. Rendell stood and then gestured with his hand for the man to have a seat. He nodded and then had a seat in front of Rendell's desk. "Mr. Murphy, I'm FBI Agent Rick Alexia…I'm here to talk to you about your wife, Journee Murphy." Rendell sat back down in his chair and then leaned back in it; he stared at the agent and was confused about what this was about. "My wife? What's this in regards to?" Agent Alexia nodded and then sat forward in his chair. "I'm just gonna get to the point, Mr. Murphy…I know your wife and it's imperative that I speak to her. Can you tell her to give me a call?"

Rendell leaned his head to the side and frowned. "What does the FBI want with my wife and how do you know her?" Rendell was now suspicious. Agent Alexia stared at Rendell and then shook his head. He couldn't give all details to Rendell about what was going on but could relay a few. "I met her five years before; I helped her and then lost contact with her. It's imperative that I speak to Jaeda."

Rendell nodded and then sighed. He was rocking back and forth in his chair and then stopped. Although he didn't know what was going on, he wanted to tread lightly with his questions and responses to the agent. "She left me and returned to her fiancé she had before we met." Agent Alexia frowned and then abruptly stood from his chair; he stared at Rendell with his mouth slightly open. "What the…she went back to Devonte Sampson? Why'd she do that…what did you do to her?" Rendell was becoming irritated with the agent's aggressive tone towards him. He stood from his chair, as he stared at the agent. "I didn't do a damn thing to my wife; she left me and after I found her, she gave me a story about amnesia and not remembering our last five years together or our son. She blew me off and said this Devonte guy was the love of her life and who she remembered. I haven't seen her in over a month so you're wasting your time talking to me."

Agent Alexia sighed and then nodded; he grabbed his cell phone off his hip and then walked away from Rendell's desk while attempting to make a call. As he did this, Rendell stopped him. Agent Alexia turned around with the cell phone to his ear; Rendell came around his desk and walked closer to Agent Alexia. "Is she uh, is Jaeda, in trouble or something?" Agent Alexia told who he had on the phone to hold on and then removed the cell phone from his ear; he sighed and then shook his head. "No, she's not in trouble…she's in danger." Before Rendell could speak, Agent Alexia continued with his call and then left Rendell's office.

Rendell stood there and then looked to the side, as he tried to process what could be going on with Jaeda and the situation she was in. He knew that he lied about the last time he saw Jaeda, but he didn't want to reveal that information to the agent. Rendell decided to try to get in contact with Jaeda again, even though they had closure and were no longer in each other's life. Regardless, he still loved her and needed to know that she was safe.

Chapter 22

Later that night, Rendell was back at home after he picked up Ju from daycare. He was happy that his sister came over to cook for all of them; her cooking wasn't in comparison to Jaeda's, but it was edible.

Rydell was in the kitchen and speaking with his aunt, when Rendell entered and greeted them with Ju in tow. Rendell had an unsettling look on his face and Meela asked him if he was alright. Rendell looked at his sister and then sighed. "No, I'm not alright…there's something going on with Journee, I mean, Jaeda; an FBI agent came to see me today and said she's in danger. We cut ties again for good, so I just hope she's alright." Rydell and Meela looked at each other and then back to Rendell. Rydell had something to speak to his dad about and was waiting until he came home but thought now wasn't the right time. He had sat there and chatted with his aunt while he waited.

Meela sat down and then sighed, as she looked at her brother. "Look Ren, I know what I said to you before about this thing with Journee, but maybe I was wrong. I mean, I watch you almost every day and since she left, you're not even happy anymore." Rendell slightly smiled at his sister and then went over to give her a hug. Afterwards, he pulled back from Meela and looked at her. "Don't worry about me…I'm fine; I'll handle this myself so don't worry." Meela nodded and then told Rendell there was food in the oven; she then said she would give Ju his bath and feed him.

Meela exited the kitchen with Ju; Rendell and Rydell were left in the kitchen. Rendell had lost his appetite, so he was about to get something to drink when he noticed the look on his son's face. "Are you alright, son?" Rendell walked to the refrigerator, as Rydell looked at his dad. "Uh nah, dad; I was gonna wait for another time, but I'ma go ahead and tell you. You remember that chick I was talking to last year?" Rendell's back was to his son because he was in the process of getting something to drink out the refrigerator. When he heard the question, he stopped what he was doing, and then slowly turned around to face his son. "Yes, I remember…why, Dell? Why? If you're about to tell me what I think you are, then I don't wanna hear it."

Rydell sighed and then stood from the stool he was sitting on. "Come on, dad…I already know you don't wanna hear this shit, but it's mine; the baby boy is mine and she even named him after me, so there it is.

He's seven months now…" Rendell closed the refrigerator and then rubbed his hands down his face. This was something that Rendell didn't need right now, but his apparent grandson was already here, so there was nothing he could do about it. Rydell waited for his dad to say something, but no words ever came out his dad's mouth. Rendell just wanted to go to bed now and reflect on everything that was going on in his life and with his family. Rendell walked past his son and then exited the kitchen. Rydell stood there and slightly threw his hands up; he expected this disappointed reaction from his dad. Rydell decided to give his dad some time to soak in all of this before speaking to him again.

Chapter 23

About time night fall hit, Jaeda was at Camille's apartment and settled in; for how long, wasn't evident to her. The one thing that Jaeda did know was that she had nowhere else to go. There was a knock, on Camille's door, and Jaeda turned her head; Camille walked out from down the hall and to her front door. She looked through the peephole and then saw that it was her brother, Devonte. Camille jogged to the living room and told Jaeda to go down the hall to the bedroom. Jaeda quickly got up and then went to the bedroom. Camille waited and then went back to the front to open the door for her brother. After she did, Devonte barged in and pushed by his sister.

Camille rolled her eyes and then closed the door; when she turned around, she faced her brother. "What the hell do you want?" Devonte stared at his sister with an unwelcoming look. "Jaeda is gone again; I don't even know the reason this time, but I need her back. She's not answering her damn phone either." Camille raised an eyebrow and then walked away from her brother. He saw the look on her face and then grabbed her arm to stop her. She turned and looked at him. "Let go of my damn arm, Devonte…" He leaned his head to the side, as he stared at her, and then shook his head. "Have you seen, Jaeda, lately? I mean, have you talked to her?" Camille snatched her arm from him and then sarcastically laughed. "Get the fuck out of here, Devonte; no, I hadn't talked to Jaeda. She don't even know who the fuck I am, so how am I gonna talk to her?"

Devonte looked to the side and then nodded. He rubbed his hands down his face and then walked around his sister to head to the living room. He was about to sit down on the couch when he heard something. He jerked his head towards the hall and then looked at his sister. "What was that? You got somebody in here?" Camille looked down the hall and then back to her brother; she shook her head. "Nobody's here…you need to go, Devonte." Camille walked back to the front, as he slightly nodded his head. He was about to follow her when he changed his direction and went down the hall.

Camille thought her brother was behind her, but when she turned around, she saw that he wasn't. She frowned and then walked back towards the living room; she heard yelling and then ran down the hall.

Devonte had gone down the hall and to his sister's closed bedroom door; he opened it and came face to face with Jaeda. She immediately started to yell at him to get away from her and then pushed him out of her way to run out the bedroom. Devonte lost his balance and hit the wall, but immediately got back on track and ran down the hall after Jaeda. "Baby, what's wrong with you!" Camille cursed to herself and then met Jaeda halfway but ran around her and to Devonte to stop him from getting to Jaeda. Jaeda was about to run out the apartment, but then turned around to see that Devonte had pushed Camille out the way and was headed for her.

Devonte yelled. "Jaeda, come here!" Camille turned around and then jumped on Devonte's back; he swung around with his sister on his back while yelling at her. Camille yelled at Jaeda. "Get the fuck out of here!" Jaeda wanted to run out but didn't want to leave Camille with Devonte; she wanted to help, so ran back over to them. While she was in the process of doing that, Devonte threw his sister off his back and then went down to grab her throat with his hands. Jaeda was horrified since she had never seen this violent side of Devonte before.

As Camille clawed at her brother's hands, while gasping for air, Jaeda went over and then tried to stop him from choking the life out of Camille. As she was hitting Devonte, he let go of Camille's throat, and then aimed his anger towards her, since she was the intended target. Camille laid on the floor of the apartment, while lifeless; she was dead.

Devonte pushed Jaeda back and then punched her in the face. She hit the wall and then went down to the floor. As he was about to grab Jaeda and pull her up from the floor, she kicked him in between his legs. Devonte grabbed himself and then went down to his knees; he yelled in pain and Jaeda used this as her opportunity to make a run for it. As she was about to run out the apartment, she looked back and saw the dead Camille on the floor. She shook her head with tears in her eyes and knew Camille's death was her fault. Jaeda grabbed Camille's car keys and then glanced at Devonte one last time before running out the apartment and to her car.

After Jaeda left the apartment complex, she continued to drive and look in the rearview mirror at the same time, just in case she was being followed. She cried silently to herself the entire time for Camille and what she had witnessed Devonte do. If Devonte wanted her dead before, then she for sure knew that he would stop at nothing to kill her now. Jaeda didn't know where she was going but knew what she had to do. She had to stop by the bank and withdraw all her money; afterwards, she had to get out of town.

Jaeda hit the highway right after she withdrew all her money from the bank; she headed towards the only other place she knew which was Houston, Texas. Even though she wasn't familiar with the city, as she assumed, she once was, she did know that she would most likely be safer there than in Atlanta.

Jaeda had been on I-10 for many hours now; it was late and close to eight that night now. She had another six hours before she reached Houston and was getting tired. She didn't want to risk it and stop anywhere for the night, so she planned to make the full drive for the remainder of the night.

While driving, her cell phone rang and she took it from her console to see who it was; she didn't recognize the number and was unsure if she should answer the call but took the chance anyway. She pressed the talk button and slightly hesitated. "Hello." Jaeda slightly frowned, as she listened to the man on the other end. Of course, she didn't or couldn't remember who he was, but he did state that he was an FBI agent and knew who she was. He stressed how important it was that he spoke to her in person.

Jaeda shook her head, no, even though he couldn't see her. "No, I can't do that…just leave me alone." She was about to end the call when he briefly told her that he helped her escape Devonte five years before. She frowned and knew now that he was telling the truth about who he was and how he knew her. She told him that she was driving and on her way to Houston; she stated how much longer she had and he said he would meet her there. She said, alright, and then ended the call. Shortly after, she received a text of where she needed to go after she arrived in Houston. Jaeda sighed and then continued on her semi-long drive to Houston.

Chapter 24

After Jaeda ran out the apartment, Devonte got himself together and then got up from the floor; the front door was still open but too much time had passed, so he knew that Jaeda was gone. He was breathing hard when he looked around and then down to his dead sister on the floor. He wiped the sweat from his forehead and then put his hand behind the back of his head. He shook his head at what he had done to her but felt that he wouldn't have had to kill Camille if she hadn't lied to him and got in his way. He dropped his hand and then pulled his cell phone from his pocket; he made a quick call because he needed the mess he made to be cleaned up once again.

After he finished his call, he closed the front door and then locked it. He then went to sit down on the couch in the living room and wait for his friend to arrive to help him dispose of his sister's body; he had to come up with a plan to find Jaeda.

After some time, Devonte was back at his apartment; he was sitting on the couch while Stone was on the adjacent couch and staring at him. Devonte lifted his head to see the stare. "What, man?" Stone slowly shook his head from side to side. "You not too good with plans, are you?" Devonte rolled his eyes and then got up from the couch to get a drink. He returned from the kitchen with a beer and then sat back down on the couch. He looked at Stone. "I'll find her so don't worry…I got an idea of where she might go, but I'm not for sure. Either way, I'll handle it." Stone rolled his eyes and didn't believe a word that Devonte just said. "The only reason I didn't kill your ass a long time ago was because you're with my sister and Corrina claims she loves you."

Devonte stared at Stone and frowned. Before he could speak, Stone did again. "I cut this deal with you, so you can keep your life, not so you could jerk me around for five damn years. That bitch was supposed to die and you were supposed to pay me with that fucking life insurance money but she's still alive, and now missing again. I can't help you no more, Devonte; I don't give a fuck if you're with my sister or not, I'ma be back to collect for the full amount next week, so if you don't have all my money then I'ma dispose of you and Corrina if she get in my fucking way."

Stone stood from the couch and looked down at Devonte, as he stared up at him. He knew that Stone was serious and if Devonte ran, then he would be found much quicker than Jaeda would. Devonte nodded his head indicating that he understood. Stone nodded in return once he knew that he and Devonte were on the same page now. He said he was leaving and when he would be back.

After Stone left the apartment, Devonte sat back against the couch and stared at the wall. He had to do something and fast, but Stone was right because he wasn't good at plans and had been messing up since day one. Killing someone for life insurance wasn't the brightest plan and it was obvious that it wasn't a well thought out plan on his part. Devonte decided that he would have to get together as much money of his own that he could and come up with a new plan before next week to get Stone the money. In the meantime, he would attempt again to look for Jaeda.

Chapter 25

It was close to midnight, in Houston, and Jaeda was dead tired but had to stay focused on what she was doing. She reached the hotel parking lot where Agent Alexia told her to meet him. His flight had already landed in Houston and he was there at the hotel, while waiting for Jaeda to arrive. Jaeda parked in front of the hotel and then grabbed her cell phone before exiting her car. She went around and then grabbed a bag out the back seat to take with her inside the hotel. She looked around while paranoid and then hurried inside. She bypassed everyone and everything to head to the elevator. After a few moments on the elevator, she exited and then looked around as she walked down the hall. Jaeda reached the door of where she was to go and then knocked.

The door shortly opened and Agent Alexia greeted her; he hurried her inside and then stuck his head out to look both ways down the hall. Afterwards, he closed the door and then locked it. He turned back around to Jaeda and then told her to make herself comfortable. She nodded and then set her bag down on the floor; she sat down at the table in the room and waited for Agent Alexia to speak again. He offered her a drink and she accepted; while he was getting her the drink, she went back over to her bag to get her cigarettes out. Afterwards, she returned to the table and lit a cigarette, as he set the glass of alcohol in front of her.

Agent Alexia sat down on the chair across from her and then sighed. "Jaeda…tell me why? Why did you really go back to Devonte? I mean, I went to see your husband and asked what happened, but he said you had amnesia." Jaeda frowned, as she blew smoke out her nose. "You went to see my husband? Who, Mr. Murphy, I mean, Rendell?" Agent Alexia nodded and Jaeda sighed; she didn't know what was going on but decided to answer all questions that he had and ask a few of her own. "He's right, I do have amnesia, at least I did…I mean, I don't remember my life with Rendell, but I do remember my life with Devonte, so when I got my memory back, I went back to Atlanta to Devonte. I only remember going to the bank that day, five years ago, and then waking up in a house and city I didn't know. Camille said I was being chased and that's what caused my accident; that must of been how I lost my memory in the first place."

Agent Alexia sighed and then nodded. "Ok, I believe you, but know that you're in danger now that you returned to Devonte and he knows you're alive."

Jaeda nodded and was aware of that now; she made a sarcastic sound and then continued to smoke her cigarette. She thought the agent's words were an understatement.

Agent Alexia stared at her. "Jaeda…Camille was an informant for the FBI at the time; we had surveillance on Devonte for a couple of years, at the time. We knew what was going on at that sandwich shop and we were only a couple of months away from raiding it when everything happened with you and we had to back off. Camille said Devonte owed money to a dealer named Stone and planned to kill you for the life insurance to pay him back." Jaeda stared at Agent Alexia as if he were telling her a horrific fairytale; she couldn't believe her ears and that Devonte was involved in what he was. The fact that he was willing to have her killed was even more astonishing and painful to her.

Agent Alexia knew this was hard for Jaeda to hear since it seemed it was the first time, she was aware of all this, but had to continue. "We were given a later day that this was supposed to happen, by Camille, but something changed. I'm still not sure what happened that day, but Camille called me and said she had you; she said you crashed your car and I needed to just get you out of town. She drove you to Decatur and that's where I met up with her and you. I took over from there and set you up with another identity so that you'd be safe. I sent you down here to Houston and made sure you were good to start your new life. I stayed in contact with you but then your phone was disconnected and that was it."

Jaeda swallowed down her drink and then set her glass back down on the table; she shook her head and then sniffed. She then wiped her eyes and looked at Agent Alexia. She shrugged her shoulders. "I don't know what to say; I don't remember any of that but it's irrelevant now anyway. I don't have nobody that I can trust and I don't have any family that I can remember to go to for help. What the hell am I supposed to do now?" She started to silently cry and Agent Alexia sighed; he stood from his chair and then walked over to her. He pulled Jaeda up and then let her cry into his chest. "Don't worry, Jaeda…I'm here to help you so you're not alone and you can trust me." Jaeda pulled back from Agent Alexia and slightly nodded her head, as he smiled at her.

Agent Alexia told her to take a shower and get herself situated; he wanted her to get some sleep and not worry about anything else tonight. She nodded and then grabbed her bag; she went to the bathroom and then shut the door. Agent Alexia put his hand behind the back of his head and then went to sit down on the bed. He had already taken his shower and was waiting for Jaeda to get out the bathroom now.

After some time passed, the bathroom door opened and Jaeda exited; she walked over to the bed and he stood from it. "I'll sleep on the couch and you can take the bed." He was about to walk away when she stopped him; he turned around to her. "This is your room so you take the bed; believe me I don't care, I just wanna go to sleep." He insisted she take the bed and she frowned; she threw her hands up. "Look, the bed is big enough for both of us, so I'll sleep under the covers and you can sleep on top with a blanket. Either that or

I'ma get on the damn floor and go to sleep." Agent Alexia gave in and said, alright, since he didn't want her on the couch or on the floor. Both got in the bed and got situated; afterwards, they both fell asleep rather quickly.

Chapter 26

It was the next day when Jaeda finally woke up; she rose in the bed and then looked at the time on the nightstand. She realized that she had slept almost all day. She sighed and then got out of bed; as she was doing this, the hotel room door opened and Agent Alexia walked in. He closed the door behind him and had two bags of food in his hands. She greeted him and then went to the bathroom to get herself together while he put the food on the table. He sat down and got his food out to eat; she exited the bathroom and then went over to the table to join him.

After she sat down, he looked at her. "Did you get enough sleep?" She grabbed her food and then looked at him. "Yeah, I guess; I thought all this was a damn dream, but after I woke up, I realized that it wasn't."

He nodded and ate his food; she did the same. As she chewed her food, she thought of something; she looked at him. "If it's money he needs then can I just get the money for him to leave me alone?" Agent Alexia frowned and then swallowed the rest of the food in his mouth; he was stunned with her question. "No, that's illegal and I'm not about to be a part of that. Besides, he tried to kill you but there's no proof that it was him. I don't know who did what that day and I can't prove he was involved; I can only go by what Camille told me. I tried to call her, but she didn't answer last night; I'll try her again." Agent Alexia grabbed his cell phone off the table and was about to call Camille again when Jaeda stopped him. He looked at her and then lowered his hand with the phone. He saw the look on Jaeda's face and knew that something was wrong. "What?"

Jaeda sighed and then looked down; she looked back up again at him and then shook her head. "She's dead…Devonte killed her; she was trying to protect me and he choked her to death, that's why I ran yesterday." Agent Alexia had his mouth open and then dropped his phone on the table. Jaeda saw the heartbroken look on his face and then saw a tear leave his eye. He quickly wiped his eye and then stood from his chair, as she followed his lead. He had his back turned to her and then she saw him look down with his hand over his face. He was quiet for too long and then Jaeda realized something. "Oh God…what was she to you?"

Agent Alexia dropped his hand and then turned around to face Jaeda; he had red eyes and a few tears were coming down his face. He cleared his throat and then swallowed hard. "Uh, she was my daughter…she and Devonte had different daddies, so she was my only child." Jaeda stepped closer to Agent Alexia and shook her head from side to side. "I'm so sorry…she was protecting me and tried to stop Devonte when he came after me yesterday. I swear, I didn't know…all this is my fault and ever since I got my memory back, bad things have been happening. Please forgive me…I'm so sorry." She put both hands to her face; he stepped closer to Jaeda and looked at her, as he removed her hands from her face. "It's not your fault, Jaeda, and I don't blame you, but we're talking about murder now along with a shit load of other charges that's waiting for Devonte when I get his ass, but I need your help." She quickly nodded her head. "Yeah, I'll do anything…" He nodded and then hugged her. She felt extremely remorseful for not doing more to save Camille's life the day before. She vowed now to make it right with at least one person and she was more than happy that person was the one helping her.

After Agent Alexia calmed himself down enough, he explained to Jaeda that no one knew that Camille was his daughter. She was an informant and both had to keep that bit of information a secret. Since Camille had her mama's last name, that wasn't hard for either of them to do. Camille didn't even tell her brother Devonte that her dad was back in her life and was an FBI agent. He asked her to help him since Camille was once close to her brother, so now Agent Alexia blamed himself for getting Camille involved in something so dangerous.

Jaeda sat there on the bed and stared at him, as he spoke. She lost both of her parents, so she knew what it felt like to lose a loved one. She comforted him as much as she could. Agent Alexia stared at Jaeda and then sighed; he realized that he couldn't get Jaeda back involved in this. He would once again be taking a risk with another innocent person's life. Since Jaeda reminded him so much of his daughter, he had made a decision. "Look Jaeda, I think I made a mistake in asking you to help me; I can't let anything happen to you like my daughter." Jaeda frowned and then shook her head, no, but he continued to protest it. "No…we might of messed up five years ago, but I guarantee that we won't mess up again. I'm gonna call this in and have everybody get ready to move on Devonte, so I want you to stay here and not leave until everything is done."

Jaeda sighed and although this wasn't what she wanted to do, she decided to follow Agent Alexia's instructions in order to keep herself safe. He smiled and then gave her a hug; afterwards, he pulled back from Jaeda and said he had to leave. He had some things to get in order and done; she understood and followed him out the hotel room to get the remainder of her bags out her car. Once outside the hotel, he told Jaeda he would keep in touch and she nodded. After she watched him leave, she went back into the hotel.

Chapter 27

It was a week later and Jaeda was still staying in the hotel that Agent Alexia provided for her; he paid the bill and kept in touch as he promised. He stressed the importance of her not being seen around the city so much and to mostly stay in the hotel room. This reason was based on the fact that Devonte Sampson had left Atlanta along with his girlfriend Corrina. Devonte Sampson was now a wanted man.

While Jaeda was watching television, there was a knock on her door; she turned her head and then got out of the bed to go over to the door. She didn't hesitate to open it, as she probably should have. She opened the door and then suddenly felt a hard blow to her face. Jaeda fell back inside the room and then hit the floor. While moaning on the floor, the door closed and then she heard it lock. She slightly shook her head while on the floor and then squint her eyes to see someone standing over her.

Jaeda felt another sharp pain coming from her head, when the man grabbed her hair and then pulled her up from the floor. She put her hands on his and winced in pain; he jerked her head towards him and then she looked at him. "Wha…what do you want?" The man grinned and then started to walk towards the bed with his hand still gripped on her hair. When he reached the bed, he flung Jaeda down and then stood over her. She yelled in pain and then looked up at him, as he spoke. "Jaeda…your boyfriend skipped out on me, so his debt is your debt now. I want the money that nigga owed me with five years' worth of interest. So, we can do this the easy way or the hard way…regardless, I'ma beat your ass with both options."

Before she could comprehend everything that he was saying, he bent down and then punched her in the face. She yelled again, as he started to pummel her with his fist. She was in dire pain and her face was bloody from the blows she was sustaining. The man beating her to a bloody pulp was Stone and he was there to collect by any means necessary.

Jaeda begged for her life and when she felt she couldn't take it anymore, she yelled that she could get him the money if he stopped. Stone stopped and then stood back from the bed, as he stared down at her. He wiped the sweat from his forehead and then grabbed the bloody Jaeda up from the bed. She silently cried out of her good eye that wasn't as bad as the other. Blood ran from her head and down her face, her left eye was swollen shut while black and blue; her lip was cut and she suspected that her nose was broken. She slowly put her hand up to him; it was a quick decision, but at this point there was only one person she could go to for help in regards to getting the money.

Jaeda sighed. "I, I know a guy that can…give me the money, for you. I need to call him…but I need…time." He shook his head. "Nah, no calls…I want whoever you getting this money from to know I'm serious and not playing. I want this person to see what can happen if he don't give up the money." Jaeda shook while slowly nodding her head; this wasn't the best situation and she just wanted Stone to stop beating her. She didn't want to involve any more people in all this, but Devonte had pulled a fast one on Stone and now Jaeda felt she had no way out. Stone told Jaeda to come with him and then drive him to where this person lived, so that he could get his money. He stressed the importance of no police and if he felt they were around and had been called, then he would kill Jaeda without flinching. Jaeda understood and shortly after, they both discreetly left the hotel.

Chapter 28

Back at the Murphy household, Meela was in the kitchen and getting ready for Rendell's thirty-fifth birthday party. Rendell wasn't in the partying mood, but Meela wanted to do this for her brother to raise his spirits and get him out of his funk. Rydell was taking care of Ju and getting him ready; Rendell was on his way home from work. He planned to take a quick shower and also get ready for his party.

While Meela was in the kitchen and finishing up with the food, Rydell walked in the kitchen. She looked at him and then shook her head; he frowned and then rolled his eyes when he realized why his aunt might be looking at him that way. "Dad told you, right?" Meela stopped what she was doing and then sighed. "Yeah, he finally told me, but I wanna know why you didn't. I can't believe you could be so damn stupid to knock up some chick." Rydell sighed and then walked over to his aunt; he sat down on the stool and then looked at her. "I know dad got a lot of other shit going on, and on his mind, but I don't want this to add on to all that. I'ma take care of my kid and I been doing that. It was stupid and I should of been more careful, but it's done and my son's already here so, it is what it is. Now Ju got somebody to play with, I guess." Meela frowned and then slightly laughed; she sighed and then told Rydell to help her finish. He nodded and then grabbed the bottles of liquor to take out to the den.

While all the finishing touches were getting done, Rendell had arrived home; he walked to the den and saw that his sister had did a good job. He thought that he should stop protesting against this party and instead enjoy himself tonight for his family's sake. Rendell walked out the den and then made his way through the house to head upstairs. He passed by Meela and thanked her for tonight; he then stated he was going to take a shower and get ready. She nodded and then took Ju in the playroom. Not too long after, the doorbell rang and the guests started to arrive.

After some time, the guests were having a good time at the house; music was playing and some were dancing, as others were either eating, drinking, or talking. Rydell had his seventeen-year-old baby mama there with their seven-month-old son. She was in the game room with Ju and keeping the children entertained with Rydell. Meela had invited the guy that she was involved with, to the party, and they were dancing.

While this was going on, Rendell turned his head when he saw two men walking towards him. He slightly laughed and then shook his head when the men approached him. The guys smiled and then shook hands with Rendell. "Mr. Campbell…Mr. Ford, I didn't expect to see you two here. Still trying to rub out the competition or is this another merger talk?" Dimitri rolled his eyes, as Jordan laughed and then shook his head. Jordan was twenty-seven and Dimitri was twenty-eight years old; they were partners at their own law firm. They had only been on their own for three years, but felt they were doing well enough to merge with a larger firm; they were very much interested in merging with Rendell's law firm.

Dimitri Campbell and Jordan Ford were Rendell's protégés. The men also worked at Rendell's law firm as interns at one point. Although flattered that the guys wanted to merge with him, he felt they just weren't ready, but stayed in touch and remained friends.

Dimitri shook his head. "Whatever, Ren…what the hell do we look like, hitmen? Meela told us about the party, so we wanted to wish your old ass a happy birthday." The guys laughed, as Rendell frowned. "Right…anyways, where are the wives?" Dimitri looked at Jordan and then back to Rendell. "At home; we both have some things going on at home right now, so we just wanted to be out without them tonight." Rendell nodded and was about to ask Dimitri what he was talking about, when his doorbell rang. He excused himself and then made his way out the den and to the front.

After Rendell was gone, Jordan looked at Dimitri. "Have some things going on at home? How subtle, Dimitri." Dimitri rolled his eyes. "It's not like I was lying. Besides, he won't pry so I'm not worried about any questions he has when he gets back." Jordan nodded. "Let's hope not. I came to relax, not talk about my marriage." Dimitri frowned. "Keep your voice down, Jordan." Jordan sighed and then the men went to grab a drink before Rendell returned.

Chapter 29

When Rendell reached the front door, he opened it to find a horrific scene. He was speechless when he saw Jaeda and the condition she was in: the same condition she was in right after Stone beat her. He didn't clean her up and wanted her to stay looking the way she was in order to prove a point.

Rendell looked at the guy standing right next to Jaeda and noticed his tight grip on her arm; he knew something was wrong. "What the hell is this, Jaeda? What happened to you?" Stone interrupted Rendell and then tightened his grip on Jaeda's arm. "Rendell Murphy, right?" Rendell nodded his head and Stone smiled. "Good…Mr. Murphy we need to talk…now; I see you got a shit load of cars outside, so I'm guessing you got a party going on here. We can either talk in private or in front of all your guests." Rendell put his hand up to Stone and understood; he said, all that wasn't necessary and he would accommodate his apparent demand.

Rendell stepped to the side; Stone walked in and Jaeda had to be dragged in by him. Rendell closed the door and swallowed hard; it was hard to see Jaeda this way. He wanted to call the police, but it seemed as if that wouldn't be the smartest thing to do right now. Rendell looked around and then told Stone to follow him to his office down the hall; Rendell didn't want anyone to see Stone or Jaeda this way.

Once in the office, Rendell closed the door and then turned around to Stone. "Alright, what's this about?" Stone pushed Jaeda down to the floor, and Rendell yelled. "What the hell!" Rendell was about to lunge at Stone, when the gun was pulled out and aimed at Jaeda's head. Rendell stopped and then slightly stepped back from Stone; he looked down at Jaeda and then back to Stone. "Alright, I'm backing off; just don't hurt her." Stone grinned and felt he was now back in charge. He jerked his head towards the couch in the office and for Rendell to have a seat. Rendell complied and then sat down; he looked at the gun, that was now drawn on him. Stone used his other hand to grab Jaeda's hair and then pulled her up from the floor; she winced in pain and Rendell felt helpless. "Stop! Just tell me what you want."

Stone looked from Jaeda and then to Rendell. "She owes me money and said I can get it from you, so I'm here to collect. I'm not leaving until I get all my money…and if you think I won't kill this bitch then try me." Stone was very serious. Rendell shook his head from side to side. He looked at Jaeda and was now concerned about what she had gotten herself into; in his mind, he felt it had to do with drugs. Since Rendell didn't know anything about Jaeda's past with Devonte, he didn't know whether she was into drugs or not.

Rendell looked back at Stone. "How much?" Stone grinned. "Two hundred and fifty thousand dollars…" Rendell almost swallowed his tongue, as he stared at Stone. He was certain now that this had to do with drugs. "Are you fucking insane? Where do you want me to pull that money out of, my ass?" Rendell was mad, but Stone wasn't playing. He tightened his grip on Jaeda, and then slammed the gun into her face. Rendell quickly stood from the couch; Jaeda yelled in pain and then Stone flung her down to the floor.

Stone aimed the gun at Rendell when he was about to react to the brutal assault on Jaeda. Rendell put his hands up and then looked down at Jaeda; he looked back at Stone. "Please, just stop…don't hurt her anymore. I'll get you the money, but I need some time; it's Friday night and the banks are closed." Jaeda tried to get up and was now on all fours; she looked up at Rendell. "Don't…don't do it, I'm…sorry." Stone turned his head to Jaeda and then kicked her in the stomach, while still aiming the gun at Rendell. She fell back down to the floor and held her arms around her stomach, while in pain. Rendell was horrified, as he watched Jaeda be beaten to an almost unrecognizable condition.

Stone looked back at Rendell. "Ok, Mr. Murphy…hit the bank tomorrow morning and call Jaeda's phone after you get it. She's coming with me and I guarantee if you call the cops I'ma kill her with no hesitation. There's only one thing I hadn't done to her yet while she's still alive, so maybe I'll get a little taste tonight before we meet tomorrow." Rendell frowned and then shook his head, no. "Look, just…I'll do it and get the money in the morning, I promise, but just don't hurt her anymore and don't touch her; she's my wife…"

Stone frowned and then leaned his head to the side; he was confused as to how Jaeda was Rendell's wife, since Devonte never mentioned this information to him before. A devious smile came across Stone's face; he was positive he would get his money now and that no police would be called. "Well, this night just keeps getting better and better; if you love this bitch and wanna see her alive tomorrow, then have my fucking money." Stone put the gun back underneath his shirt; he then reached down and pulled Jaeda up from the floor. He told Rendell not to leave the office for five minutes. Rendell nodded and agreed. Tears fell from his eyes when he made eye contact with the beaten Jaeda; she mouthed that she was sorry. He watched, as Stone dragged Jaeda out the office; they were out of sight. Rendell slowly started to walk towards the door and then looked out to see if Stone and Jaeda were still visible. He then walked out the office to go find his sister.

As Stone had Jaeda and made his way towards the front door, Rydell saw and then frowned. He stopped the suspicious guy and as Stone and Jaeda turned around, Rydell's eyes grew big. "What the fuck!" He saw the condition Jaeda was in. Rendell heard his son and quickly ran the rest of the way to the front; he stopped at his son and then pulled him back. He put his hand up to Stone and told him to leave. He reassured Stone that he would have the money in the morning. Stone quickly dragged Jaeda out the front door and then they were gone.

Chapter 30

After Stone and Jaeda were gone, Rydell looked at his dad. "What the fuck was that about? Did you see her? Who was that dude?" Rendell told his son to keep his voice down and Rydell was dumbfounded that his dad was so nonchalant about this. The woman he claimed he loved and was technically still married to, had just been dragged out the house by an unidentified man, while looking as if she had been beaten all day.

Rendell sighed. "There's something going on and I need to handle it tomorrow; I don't know all the details, but that guy said Jaeda owed him money and I need to pay it or he'll kill her. I can't call the police and from what I've seen I wouldn't do that anyway. I just…" Rendell stopped talking and then rubbed his hands down his face; he was drained mentally and physically. He dropped his hands and had almost forgotten that he had guests in the den celebrating his birthday.

Rydell was confused about what his dad just said. "How much money, dad?" Rendell looked at his son and then sighed. "Two hundred and fifty thousand…" Rydell had his mouth open and couldn't believe any of this; from the way his dad was looking at him, it was evident that he was going to pay. Rydell shook his head. "Dad, come on…you're not gonna pay that dude, are you?" Before he could answer, Meela walked over to them; she wondered where her brother went and had sent Rydell to find him. When Rydell never returned, she left the party to go find the guys. When she did, she frowned when she saw the look on their faces. "What's wrong?" Rydell was going to tell his aunt what was happening, but Rendell interjected. "Nothing is wrong, Meela; apologize to my guests because I'm heading upstairs."

Rydell looked at his dad as if he lost his mind and then both he and his aunt watched as Rendell walked around them to head upstairs. After Rendell was gone, Meela looked at Rydell and asked her nephew what was going on; he sighed and then told her. Afterwards, Meela was mad, so she told Rydell to get back to the guests and she would speak to Rendell. He nodded and then both went their separate ways.

Meela made her way upstairs and then to Rendell's bedroom; she knocked on the door and heard him say to go away. She ignored her brother and opened the door anyway; he was sitting on the bed and looked up to see his sister. He sighed and told Meela to leave him alone. She once again ignored him and closed the door behind her, before walking further into the bedroom. Meela walked over to her brother and then shook her head at him. "What the hell is wrong with you? Dell told me what's going on…are you seriously gonna pay them? You don't even know that guy that she was with, so he's probably some guy she's fucking and they're trying to extort money from you. I mean…" Rendell abruptly stood from the bed. "Shut the fuck up, Meela!" She stopped talking and stared at her brother.

Rendell put his hand over his face and then dropped it. "From what I saw, nobody is trying to extort a damn thing. He beat the shit out of her right in front of me…hard blows, not little playful taps, so whatever is going on is serious and she was sucked into it." Meela sighed and then turned her head to the side; she looked back at her brother and then shrugged her shoulders. "Alright, but where are you gonna get the money from?" Rendell slightly moved his eyes to the side and Meela frowned; she leaned her head to the side, as she stared at him. "Ren…where are you gonna get the money from?" He looked at her and then cleared his throat. "I'm gonna use Dell's college fund." Meela stood there with her mouth open and then vigorously shook her, no. "You can't do that…that's for his tuition; he's gonna be pissed at you, Ren. He already said he thinks they're trying to scam you, so he's never gonna talk to you again if you do this."

Rendell put his hand behind the back of his head and felt helpless now. That would be the easiest way to retrieve the money in the morning; the hard way would take some time, which is what he didn't have. He dropped his hand and then sighed, as he looked at his sister. "What do you want me to do, Meela? I don't know what to do and I don't know what to believe, but she's still my wife..." Meela shook her head and didn't know what to tell him. She started to speak again and he ignored her; he thought of something and then told his sister to be quiet. Meela stopped talking and stared at her brother; it looked as if he had something else on his mind now. Rendell looked around and then told Meela he knew what to do now but for her not to worry or tell Rydell anything. She wasn't sure what her brother was going to do now but she complied.

Meela said she was going back to the party and he nodded; he said he would be back down shortly. After Meela left the bedroom, Rendell took his cell phone from his hip and then made a call.

Chapter 31

Back at the hotel, Jaeda was barely hanging on; both slipped back in the hotel without being seen. They were in the room and Stone was sitting at the table, while Jaeda was on the floor and in fetal position; she didn't move while thinking that he would start beating her again. While lying on the floor, she thought about her life, the part that she could remember. She then started thinking about something else that popped into her head.

Jaeda was facing Stone while he was at the table, so she looked at him. She didn't want Rendell to pay Stone anything but it seemed he would pay anything to keep her safe. Jaeda weakly spoke. "Can I have some water?" He looked at her and then sighed. Stone got up from the table and then went to the mini refrigerator to see what was in it. He found a bottle of water and then closed the refrigerator before he took it to her. When he reached her, he knelt down to give her the water and that's when Jaeda made her move. She used all her strength and lunged forward to bite his neck. He yelled in pain; Jaeda's teeth had a good grip on the flesh from his neck. She was like a pit bull who hadn't eaten in weeks. He yelled more and tried to get her off of him but failed; Jaeda finally pulled back and had a big chunk of his flesh in her mouth. She spit it out along with blood; his eyes grew big and he fell back onto the floor.

Stone was bleeding profusely; he had his hands to his neck to stop all the blood that was spewing out. Jaeda got up and then grabbed her keys from the table; she then ran out the hotel room, as Stone tried to get up from the floor. Jaeda was gone, but Stone had enough strength where he could get up. He quickly went to the bathroom and then took a towel to wrap around his neck to stop the blood. When he was finished, he was sweating profusely and becoming weak. He stumbled out the bathroom and then looked around; he started to pat himself and then found his keys in his pocket. Stone ran out the room to go after Jaeda.

*   *   *

Jaeda was still in pain while she drove; she was also crying and scared to death of what she had just done. She still had Stone's blood in and around her mouth. She could have called the police but she didn't; she felt that would have made the situation even worse. She didn't have her cell phone anyway, so she couldn't call anyone. Jaeda wiped her face with her forearm as she drove and decided to hide out for the remainder of the night until she was able to get to a phone or return to Atlanta. Jaeda found a dead-end road and then parked; she didn't have much gas left in her car, so she decided not to waste anymore. She turned the car off and then sat back in the seat. She looked around and didn't know where she was but it was irrelevant at the moment. As long as she was nowhere near Stone then she felt safe.

Chapter 32

It was the next morning and Rendell was at home; he couldn't sleep at all the previous night, so was already up, while still thinking about what to do. He was also waiting for someone to arrive that he thought could help.

Rydell was in the living room with his dad, and Meela had taken Ju with her overnight to her apartment. The doorbell rang and Rendell stood from the couch, before he walked out the living room. When Rendell reached the front door, he opened it and then stepped aside, as Agent Alexia walked in. After the door was closed, Agent Alexia turned around to Rendell. "Where is she? What happened?" Agent Alexia was anxious to know.

Rendell sighed. "Look, I don't know what's fully going on, but…" Agent Alexia put his hand up to stop him, as he interjected. "I don't wanna hear that. I had her in a hotel room and you tell me she showed up last night all beaten and with an unknown guy. Now tell me where she is?" Rendell had no idea of that extra information, so he nodded and agreed to tell the agent what he knew so far. He told the agent to follow him to the living room.

Once in the living room, Rydell looked up and the men sat down. Agent Alexia leaned forward on the couch and waited. Rendell nodded. "Yes, she was beaten badly and the guy said he did it; he said he'd kill her if I didn't give him the money that she owed to him. He wanted two hundred and fifty thousand, but there's no way I can get that money for him right now. He said to call her phone when I had it…after I went to the bank this morning."

Agent Alexia stood from the couch and then put his hand behind his head; he turned around and paced the floor. Rydell frowned and was still disgusted with all of this. He angrily stood from the couch. "I know it's a damn scam; that dude with the tattoo on his neck looked like some dude she was probably fucking and they both decided to extort money from my dad." Agent Alexia dropped his hand and then turned around to look at Rydell. "A tattoo? What was the tattoo of?"

Rydell looked at his dad and then back at Agent Alexia. "A cross…" Agent Alexia shook his head and was mad. "Jaeda is not scamming anyone and that guy is very dangerous; the reason she had to run in the first place is because Devonte Sampson wanted her dead for the insurance money, but he failed. I helped her start over with a new identity, but she must have lost her memory before she left Atlanta, so she returned to Devonte when she got her memory back, not knowing that she put herself back in danger. Now he's missing and wanted by us, and the guy Devonte owed the money to, must want Jaeda to pay for the botched attempt on her life five years ago. She watched my daughter get killed by Devonte right in front of her…she's like a daughter to me, so I'm gonna do everything I can to protect her whether you two believe all this or not."

Rydell had his mouth open; Rendell stood from the couch and was in disbelief, but he believed all this wasn't a scam and that she was in danger. Rydell felt bad now that he thought the worst of his stepmother. "So, what do we do?" Agent Alexia shook his head and had to think. "I don't know…I tried to call Jaeda's phone this morning and nobody answered, so something must of went wrong if he said to call her phone when you had the money and nobody's answering. I'm gonna put a trace on her cell phone; do you have a laptop I can use?" Rendell nodded and then walked with the agent to his office down the hall. When they reached the office, Rendell showed Agent Alexia his laptop and he nodded. After the laptop was opened for him, Agent Alexia got down to business; while he was typing, he was on his cell phone at the same time.

Rendell left the office and then stood in the hall; he leaned against the wall and then sighed. All of this was too much for him and he would have never dreamed that something like this could happen to his family, to his wife for that matter. After some time passed, Rendell was still in the hall and daydreaming when Agent Alexia came out the office. He stopped at Rendell and he looked at him. "Something is wrong…her cell phone was tracked back to the hotel room where she's supposed to be, but she's not answering her phone. I just got a call and her car was found abandoned on a dead-end street. I sent someone to the hotel room and the police are now there; there's blood everywhere and nobody is there. It's now a crime scene until either Jaeda or Steven 'Stone' Verio are found. I guess you don't have to worry about paying that money anymore." Agent Alexia walked away from Rendell and then left the house, since there was no reason for him to stay any longer; he had to get to the hotel.

Rendell stood there while in a daze of what he was just told. He thought about his family, especially his children. He wanted to think of happy thoughts now since it was a possibility that his wife was dead, so he thought about the first time they met and it made him slightly smile.

Rydell found his dad in the hall after Agent Alexia left and confronted him about what was going on now. Rendell looked at his son. "She might be dead… that's what's going on now." Rendell walked away from his son and then went upstairs; Rydell sighed and then shook his head.

Chapter 33

Five years later…

Rendell was in his office and working when there was a knock at his door. He told whoever it was to enter; he stopped what he was doing, as the door opened. Dimitri Campbell and Jordan Ford entered; they closed the door behind them. Rendell sat back against his chair and looked at the men; he gestured for them to have a seat and they did. Dimitri and Jordan hadn't spoken to or seen Rendell in five years, not since his thirty-fifth birthday party. It was more so due to how busy Dimitri and Jordan were, as well as everything that Rendell had going on in his life.

Dimitri looked at Jordan and then back to Rendell. "So, what's this about, Mr. Murphy?" Rendell rolled his eyes with Dimitri's formality. "I called you two in because I'm ready to merge; I've watched you two over the years and I think age comes with wisdom. You're both over thirty now and I've seen good work, so I wanna know if you two are on board?" Dimitri looked at Jordan and then back to Rendell. When they first approached Rendell with a merger, they were in their infancy and Rendell had been around much longer than they had. Rendell rejected their proposition but told the men it was possible at a later date.

Jordan and Dimitri were now established and groomed their law firm to a great successful business over the past few years but felt there was always room for greater things. Dimitri cleared his throat. "Why the change of heart, Ren?" Rendell shrugged his shoulders and then sighed. "I just turned forty and as part of my midlife crisis phase, I decided to merge with you two." Jordan laughed and Dimitri rolled his eyes. The guys understood. Dimitri nodded. "Alright, Ren; well, since we made you proud over the years and we're all a success, then doing this would work out for all of us. We're on board with this, so have your people call our people, and we'll make this happen."

Rendell nodded and then stood from his chair, as Dimitri and Jordan did the same; the men all shook hands, and then Dimitri and Jordan left the office. Rendell sat back down in his chair and then rubbed his hands down his face. He had a lot on his plate these days and many changes had occurred over the course of the years.

Jaeda was never seen again and Stone's body was eventually found in his car; he had bled to death from his neck injury. Devonte Sampson had never been found but Corrina was eventually captured. At some point while on the run, Devonte ditched Corrina and left her to fend for herself; he had withdrawn all of his money and borrowed some from his parents to supposedly flee the country. Corrina was devastated that he left her behind and thought that Devonte loved her, while Devonte felt Corrina was dead weight and would only hold him back. Corrina didn't know where he was going and he hadn't fled the country yet when he ditched her, so when she was caught, she was little help to the FBI. Although Corrina had nothing to do with anything that Devonte was involved with, she was still charged with accessory after the fact, and aiding and abetting; she was given three years in prison. Since Jaeda was never seen or heard from again, the Murphy family believed that she was dead, so they had to move on. Rendell divorced Jaeda shortly after.

Rendell worked a few more hours and then started to get ready to leave. Although he, Dimitri, and Jordan were going to merge, it was still going to take some time. As he gathered his things to leave, his cell phone rang; he took it off his hip and answered on his way out of his office. He spoke for a few minutes and then ended the call; he was now on his way home.

Chapter 34

After Rendell got home, he greeted Rydell; he had recently stopped by to speak to his dad and was waiting for him. Rydell was twenty-three and graduated from college the previous year with a bachelor's degree in accounting. He worked at his dad's firm in the finance department; he was doing well in his ventures in life and was going to follow in his dad's footsteps to be a success. Since Rendell agreed to merge with Campbell & Ford, Rendell was going to keep his son in the business with him, if he wanted. Rydell Jr. was now five and a half years old and lived with his mama; everyone called him Ry.

Rendell walked through the house and then found his oldest son in the kitchen; he was sitting on a stool at the kitchen island and going through his cellphone.

Rendell set his briefcase down on the counter and then addressed his son. "Where's Meela? I thought she was coming over today and where's Ju?" Rydell looked at his dad. "I don't know where Aunt Meela at and Amelia went to pick up Ju from school." Rendell nodded and then his phone vibrated; he grabbed it off his hip and then read the text message. Rydell frowned, as he stared at his dad. He had noticed that his dad was acting strange lately but didn't know if anyone else noticed it. "You alright, dad?" Rendell looked from his phone and then to his son; he nodded and said he was fine. Before Rydell could speak, they both heard the front door.

As they waited, Amelia and Ju walked in the kitchen. Rendell greeted his son and then turned his head to his wife; he kissed her on the lips and then she said she would get dinner started. "What do y'all want to eat tonight?" Rendell looked at his son and then back to his wife; he shrugged his shoulders. "Whatever you can make, I mean, whatever you know how to cook then that's fine, baby." Rydell slightly put his head down and laughed at his dad's mishap of words, since Amelia couldn't cook but she did try. She put her hand on her hip and frowned. Rendell put his hand up and then excused himself from everyone before she said anything to him.

Amelia and Rendell met through a mutual acquaintance three years before; they dated for a year and then were married three months after. Although Rydell wasn't sure about this union, he just wanted his dad to be happy and it seemed fully moving on with his life was the best thing to do. Rendell knew getting remarried was the right thing he needed to do.

Rendell was in his bedroom and looking through his cell phone; he saw he was invited to a friend's birthday party but decided to decline. He went to take his shower and then was going to order a pizza afterwards. He usually ate lunch at work so he wouldn't have to eat when he got home, since his wife couldn't cook. He missed lunch today and was hungry. Once Rydell found out Amelia couldn't cook, he stopped coming over for dinner; Meela stopped coming for dinner as well. She would usually pick up Ju from school and feed him at her home before taking him home. It was a lot that everyone had to go through just so they didn't have to eat Amelia's cooking, but Ju got food poisoning the last time he ate his step mama's food and that was enough for Rendell not to have any of his family eat her cooking again.

After Rendell finished his shower, he sat down on the bed with his phone again and then smiled, as he stared at the blank screen. He thought about Jaeda and her restaurant style cooking. He missed her cooking and sometimes thinking about the little things in regards to her, made him smile; it most definitely made his day. He did love Amelia, but she was plan b. He felt in certain circumstances that sometimes you had to just go to 'plan b' if 'plan a' wasn't an option anymore.

Rendell sighed and then dropped his phone in his lap; he rubbed his hands down his face and then looked around the bedroom. He got up from the bed and then got dressed; he felt he needed to go out tonight.

Chapter 35

Rendell pulled into the driveway of a home and then parked; he exited his car and then looked around before walking to the front door. He rang the doorbell and then waited for a few seconds. The door opened and he smiled; he walked inside and then closed the door behind him. Rendell grabbed Jaeda and then kissed her vigorously. Afterwards, he pulled back from her. "I missed you, baby…it's been some time; I thought you forgot about me again."

Jaeda pulled back from Rendell and then shook her head. "Very funny, Ren…I hope I don't forget you again; I just had some things to do. So, you were able to get away tonight?" She started to walk to the living room while speaking, so he followed her. Once in the living room, they sat down on the couch and she lit a cigarette. He looked at her and then nodded. "I was invited to a birthday party tonight, but I declined; I told Amelia I was going, so she wouldn't expect me home anytime soon." Jaeda nodded and then sighed, as she blew smoke out her nose.

Jaeda looked down and then back up again. "So, what are we doing, Ren? I wanna see my son and you won't let me because Amelia is in the picture. You come over and get some ass like I'm your sideline and…" Rendell stopped her from talking and then frowned. "Wow, so now you think you're my sideline? Baby, you're making it sound like I'm using you or something. I love you and you used to be my damn wife, so don't ever think I'm using you or treating you like a damn whore on the side." Jaeda shook her head and then put her cigarette out; she looked at Rendell and before she spoke, he did, again. "I know you wanna see, Ju, but I don't know how to go about doing that, at least not right now. I had to tell him that you died and he hasn't seen you since he was three; he calls Amelia, mama, so…"

Jaeda stopped him and then abruptly stood from the couch; she stared at Rendell with hate in her eyes. "Are you serious? Why did you let that happen when you knew…" Jaeda stopped talking and then put her hand up; she didn't want to talk about this anymore. Jaeda nodded her head and made a decision. "Ok, well, I guess there's nothing more for me to say, so go to that birthday party or go home because I don't want nothing to do with you again."

Rendell frowned and then stood from the couch; he shook his head, no, and then stepped closer to Jaeda. "Baby, don't do this. I just got you back and I don't wanna lose you again for any reason. I told Amelia that you died too, so I'll just tell her that it was a mistake and that you want to be back in Ju's life. That'll guarantee that you can see him whenever you want with no problems. Just give me some time to get this straight with her, so there won't be any suspicion that me and you are doing something."

Jaeda nodded and agreed but was confused with one thing. "Ok, but what do you mean, suspicion of me and you doing something? Who said that this was gonna keep going?" He frowned and then pulled her even closer to him; he licked his lips, as he eyed her. "If you think I'm gonna stop making love to you then you must have amnesia again, because I'm never letting you go again. I'm still in love with you and that'll never change." Jaeda rolled her eyes and then nodded; he smiled and then kissed her.

Afterwards, he stepped back from her. "Uh, before we make love, can you please make me something to eat? I'm hungry and I haven't eaten an edible home cooked meal since I got married." Jaeda frowned and then laughed, but he was serious. He begged her to cook him anything and she laughed even harder. He rolled his eyes and she stopped. "Yeah alright, but after the bedroom…you can have your dessert first and then I'll cook you something after, if you still have your energy to eat." He grinned and then she took his hand; she escorted him to her bedroom and then afterwards, closed the door behind them.

To be continued…

Epilogue

Two years before…

The doorbell rang and Rendell jogged to the front door to see who was there. When he reached the door, he opened it and then slightly stepped back. He shook his head from side to side, as Jaeda stood there and stared at him. It had been two years since he had seen her; it was thought that she was dead. "Uh Ren, I just came to give you this." She handed a small box to Rendell and he took it; he looked at the box and then back up to her. He didn't know what to say, so he just stepped aside so she could walk in. She slightly smiled and then nodded, as she walked inside. He closed the door behind her and then she followed him to the den.

After they were in the den, they both sat down and he stared at her while in a trance. "I don't understand, Journee…uh, Jaeda…I don't get it. Agent Alexia said you disappeared again and everyone thought you were dead. What happened?" Jaeda looked down and then back up again at him. "I just had to lay low until all this was over. I didn't know if that guy was still around or Devonte, but I found out that guy was dead; they said Devonte is still missing but I know he wouldn't risk coming back in town just for me, so I thought it was time to show my face again. I just wanna say that I'm sorry again for everything I put you through."

Rendell sighed and then nodded, as he thought about the last time, he saw Jaeda in her beaten and bloody condition; he feared the worst and thought she was dead. He snapped out of his thoughts and then got back to her. "I'm not sorry, Jaeda…you were still my wife back then and I still loved you, so I would have done anything. But uh, what's this for?" He slightly raised the box to her and she smiled. She told him to open it and he did.

After he opened the box, he frowned and then took the men's watch out. "This is nice, but what is it for?" She smiled. "I missed your birthday a couple of months ago, so I just wanted to give that to you…I didn't forget your birthday." He lowered the watch and then put it back in the box. "What do you mean, you…you remember my birthday?" She nodded and he stood from the couch. She followed his lead and then he stared at her, as she spoke. "I got my whole memory back of my life with you and the boys about a year ago, but I still stayed away. Every time I come around, I just seem to make things worse with y'all, so I decided it was best to stay away for good. I'm leaving again and I'm not coming back, but I just wanted to give that to you."

Rendell frowned and was now mad. He shoved the box into her chest and she frowned this time, as he angrily spoke. "You just decided to stay away, huh? Where the hell do you get off making decisions like that when you affect everyone else's life in the process? We still have a son together that cried for his mama almost every night. It was better when we all thought you were dead and you should have just stayed away this time, and not come here to give me this damn watch. I moved on with my life and met a woman."

Jaeda flung the box on the couch and then put both hands up; she backed away from Rendell and then dropped her hands. "Ok, so I see it was a damn mistake to come here. I don't fucking get you…I get cussed out for staying away, I get cussed out for leaving, I get cussed out for coming back. What the fuck do you want from me! What can I do to make this right, Ren, because everybody is driving me crazy? I been apologizing to everybody for years, for memories that I forgot I had and now for memories that I got back." Jaeda stopped talking and then turned to leave; he cursed to himself and then followed her out the den and towards the front door.

Jaeda was about to grab the doorknob when he grabbed her arm to turn her around; she looked at him, as he stared at her. "I'm sorry, but Ju wasn't the only one that cried at night for you; I had the rest of our lives planned out. I pictured us growing old together and in a split second all of that was gone. I know I might have said some bad things to you after you lost your memory, and I'm deeply sorry for that but it hurt so much. Now you're back and I already moved on."

Jaeda sighed and then nodded; she suspected that after all this time Rendell did move on and was prepared for it when she came over today. She feared this day the most out of everything that happened to her. "Ok Ren, I get it and I know you were hurting but I'm hurting now…I lost everything; I lost family here and I lost you, so believe me when I say I'll be the one suffering from now on." She was about to turn to leave again when he stopped her once again, and turned her back around. "You didn't lose me, baby…I'm still here." Rendell pulled Jaeda to him and then kissed her passionately; she put her hand to his chest while indicating that she was going to push him back but didn't. Rendell backed her to the door and had his hands all over her. He slowly pulled back from Jaeda and then grinned. "I hope you don't think I'm letting you leave."

Jaeda frowned since she didn't understand. "Wha…what are you gonna do to me?" She was a little frightened while thinking about what Stone did to her. He nodded, as he stared at her. "I'm still in love with you and I never stopped loving you. I spent many nights dreaming about making love to you again and now I have that chance. I'm not stupid, so being mad at you right now is not gonna stop me from being in between your legs again. My fiancée is out of town, so will you stay the night with me?" Jaeda opened her mouth to speak and then closed it; she was rendered speechless but couldn't get the word out to tell him, yes.

Rendell stepped back from Jaeda and then took her hand. "I'll take that as a, yes…I love you." He pulled her away from the front door and before he turned around to head upstairs, she stopped him. "I love you too." He smiled and then turned around to go upstairs, with Jaeda in tow.

JAKLEENA 'J' WARE

Is an Independent author who currently lives in Spring, Texas, and has four children. She is a 2001 graduate of El Campo High School in El Campo, Texas. She received two Associates Degrees, in Occupational Studies for Auto Cad/Drafting and another in Applied Sciences for Paralegal. Her first series entitled, **Family Affairs**, has thirty-one volumes; her second series entitled, **The Toll Road Girls**, has twelve parts; her third series entitled, **Justified**, has twenty-eight parts; and her fourth series entitled, **Fontaine**, has thirty parts. All series are available on Amazon and Kindle. Her fifth series entitled, **Sidelines**, has seventeen parts. This is part one of the seventeen-part series.

www.ingramcontent.com/pod-product-compliance
Lightning Source LLC
Chambersburg PA
CBHW071752150726
47998CB00005B/1909